Also by Nicole Bailey-Williams

A Little Piece of Sky

Harlem Moon

Broadway Books
New York

floating

a novel

nicole bailey-williams

Published by Harlem Moon, an imprint of Broadway Books, a division of Random House, Inc.

FLOATING. Copyright © 2004 by Nicole Bailey-Williams. All rights reserved. No part of this book may be reproduced or transmitted in any form or by any means, electronic or mechanical, including photocopying, recording, or by any information storage and retrieval system, without written permission from the publisher. For information, address Broadway Books, a division of Random House, Inc.

PRINTED IN THE UNITED STATES OF AMERICA

HARLEM MOON, BROADWAY BOOKS, and the HARLEM MOON logo, depicting a moon and a woman, are trademarks of Random House, Inc. The figure in the Harlem Moon logo is inspired by a graphic design by Aaron Douglas (1899–1979).

Visit our website at www.harlemmoon.com

First edition published 2004

Library of Congress Cataloging-in-Publication Data
Bailey-Williams, Nicole.
    Floating : a novel / Nicole Bailey-Williams.—1st. ed.
      p. cm.
      1. Racially mixed people—Fiction. 2. Identity
(Psychology)—Fiction. 3. Interracial marriage—Fiction.
4. Problem families—Fiction. 5. Group identity—
Fiction. 6. Young women—Fiction. 7. Girls—Fiction.
I. Title.

PS3552.A3748F57 2004
813'.6—dc22

2003056727

ISBN 0-7679-1564-X

10 9 8 7 6 5 4 3 2 1

Dedicated to
My husband, my hero, my heart,
G.E.W.

acknowledgments

Like every other sinner who accomplishes something noteworthy, I'd like to thank God first for the gifts of life and love.

Next, my husband, my heart, my hero, Gregory E. Williams, Esq., is to be thanked for his unwavering support. Every time I think that a task is too mighty to undertake, and every time I am feeling too small to matter, my husband gently puffs air back into me, and I am big again.

My family is my lifeline. My parents, Robert and Adrean Bailey, continue to do more for me than parents should have to do. My brother, Michael, is my cheerleader who is always ready to hit the road in support of me.

My grandfather, Louis Ellis, continues to inspire me with his wisdom, and my grandmother, Irene Bailey, keeps me laughing. My godmother, Mary Patterson, is the epitome of finer womanhood. All three of these elders have put so much into me, and I feel that success is the ultimate "Thank you."

My "sister," Danielle Williams, sustains me with her silent support, listening to my crazy musings, never judging but always caring. Thanks, sister. I love you.

My "girls," Monifa Banks-Harrison, Darlise Blount, Tonya "Cracky"

Richardson, Van Robinson, and Kelley Kenner definitely keep me going with laughter, reflection, and love. My Sorors in Quaker City Alumnae Chapter of Delta Sigma Theta, especially Sonjia Stanton, Sharon Dawson-Coates, and Tracy Oliver, are thanked for their constant show of sisterhood.

My editor, Janet Hill, is phenomenal, and her vision for Harlem Moon specifically and African American literature generally should be applauded. My agent, Peter Miller, should be thanked as well. My publicist, "Lady" Laura Pillar, deserves a gold star for her endurance and optimism.

My colleague and friend Barbara Trainor is a gem whose maternal guidance keeps me focused at work. Tremendous thanks go to my student teacher, Tiffany Lynch, for holding things down during the *A Little Piece of Sky* tour.

Fellow scribes who provide marvelous support include my Soulful Sisters/Sorors Patricia Haley, Jamellah Ellis, Victoria Christopher Murray, Stephanie Perry Moore, and Nancey Wilson. Ranking right up there are Kenji Jasper, Marita Golden, Tracy Price Thompson, TaRessa Stovall, Kimberla Lawson Roby, Carol Taylor, Gloria Mallette, Bernadette Connor, Diane McKinney-Whetstone, William July, and Omar Tyree. Some other writers who have made this trip enjoyable are Sharon Mitchell, E. Lynn Harris, Mat Johnson, Benilde Little, Donna Hill, Steve Perry, Tonya Marie Evans, C. Kelly Robinson, Leslie Esdaile, Collen Dixon, and, of course, my Sorors from Delta Authors on Tour.

Numerous people in the literary and media worlds have enriched my life in many ways. In no particular order, they are Glenn R. Townes, Felicia Polk, Mondella Jones, Robin Green-Carey, Kate Garrick, Toni Short, Robert Scott Adams, Evette Porter, Adrienne Ingrum, Tamlin Henry, Peggy Hicks, Karen Grigsby Bates, Dr. Jean

Moore, Malik Ellis, Jeffrey Glass, Dr. Paula Barnes, Dr. Amee Carmines, Rob Dixon (WHOV–Hampton, VA), Lecia Warner from Basic Black in Philly, Peggy Hicks, Temi Dada, Julia Shaw, and Bill Cox. I truly thank you for your kindness.

Special thanks also go to Rick Stanton, Mrs. Cathy Moody, Soror Adrienne McMichaels, and Mrs. Carolyn Richardson.

And finally, to my student John "Hoppy" Hopkins, thanks for showing me that there's so much to know about living in two worlds.

prologue

In my father's dreams, there is no color. Only varying shades of black, and the blackness haunts him, so in every waking moment, he runs to whiteness.

That's how he met my mother.

She seemed everything that he was not. She was everything he desired. Her skin, like buttermilk, contrasted his coal color. Her hair, like corn silk, was silent while his raged. Her voice, like tiny bells, tinkled and his own boomed. She was everything that the women of his past were not, and he wanted to possess her. But like the child who cradles a wounded bird too tightly, he crushed her. Almost. In the split second it took him to reposition his hands to get a tighter hold, she saw the crack of light from the outside world and rushed toward it. Leaving him. Leaving me.

And I'm not enough for him.

My memories of them together come back to me in waves, and like waves, they threaten to drown me. But I gasp and struggle through, remembering that always there is the surface, and with the surface comes fresh air, and in the air, I am free.

part one

between

the equation

We had lived in Mt. Airy from the time I was born. The cozy community was far enough from what my father called "North Philly Nigga Shit" and close enough to chic Chestnut Hill for it to feel like a real home. Mt. Airy was a cauldron of cultures, bubbling and brimming until they became one. One common way of speaking. One common style of dress. One common way of thinking. My father believed that Mt. Airy was the place where he and my mother would live as one forever. And they did, we did, for a time.

i remember

I remember my first day of school. My mother stood on the corner of the bus stop waving to me. She looked like an angel, only she was crying. I never thought that angels cried, but when I looked into my mother's face, I knew that God's helpers shed tears from time to time.

I remember that until I started school, I lived in racial oblivion. I was just another shade in my community, just another shade in my family. Then I boarded the school bus heading toward Rush Elementary School in Chestnut Hill.

I remember marching bravely like a big girl, knowing that my mother was watching me. I wanted her to be proud, so I raised my chin like I had seen actors do in a show of bravery. I didn't know, I couldn't know, that that one act, the slight lifting of the chin, would define people's reactions to me forever. Forever. Forever different. Forever an outsider. Forever alone.

I remember that the ride to school was uneventful, yet my mind raced with anticipation. Questions about cubbyholes and midmorning snacks danced in my head as I stared out the window. So fast and furious were my thoughts that I didn't notice the furtive looks being cast my way or the fingers pointing at me. It was better that I didn't, or else I, like a crab being removed from the bushel and readied for cooking, would have sensed the impending death of my innocent spirit.

I remember approaching the morning with optimism. Sitting at my desk, I folded my hands just like my mother taught me. Every now and then I would catch some of the girls looking at me. Sometimes it was a brown girl who would grin shyly if I caught her eye. Other times, it was a tan girl who would stare game-faced, trying to decipher the puzzle that was me.

I remember lingering longer than necessary in the cubbyhole room, trying to see if anyone would invite me to play with them. After I removed my jump rope, I repacked and zipped my book bag. One of the brown girls sidled up to me.

I remember the envy in her eyes as she eyed my two dark honey-colored ponytails before saying, "You've got pretty hair."

I remember another brown girl tapping her foot impatiently. Half-disgusted, half-hateful, she snorted, "Come on, Tiffany."

Then Tiffany left, and I remember walking outside last and alone while everyone else formed Noah's Ark–like pairs ahead of me.

It was a foreshadow that would define the rest of my life.

the next day

Hope swirled in my head the next day when I awoke, and I erased thoughts of purposeful exclusion when I remembered lining up for recess and lunch. Things would be different the next day, I had assured myself before drifting into sleep.

In retrospect, I remembered the anxiety I faced at the bus stop, on the bus ride, and on the walk to the cubbyhole room before going out for recess. I wanted so badly for things to be different, but I feared that the loneliness would be a routine for me to settle into.

Then a change. A little girl, who looked all golden and fair like my mother, approached me.

"Hi," she said.

"Hi," I returned shyly.

"Do you want to play with us?" she asked, gesturing toward a small group of tan girls.

I smiled and shook my head. Gathering my rope, I fell in step beside her.

"I asked my mom if it would be okay to play with you," she said innocently. "I told her that you're almost my color, just a little darker. You aren't nearly as dirty as those other girls, so you must be one of us."

My mouth fell open as surprise overtook me.

Before I could say anything, she continued. "Besides, Heather said that she saw your mom, and she's one of us. I told my mom, and she said that at least you're half-good, so you can play with us."

My stomach quivered as I looked at my skin for signs of dirt that had somehow been branded onto me. Comparing my tanner skin to hers, I felt that my skin had been mysteriously sullied and that I was supposed to be tan like her and my mother. I ran to the bathroom where I threw up the vestiges of the bliss of old that I had formerly known. My teacher ran after me.

I was spared from recess that day by the nurse's office. I looked out the window, watching as the other kids naturally fell into groups together. Tan girls. Brown girls. Brown boys. Tan boys. As I watched, the tans became white and the browns became black. And I fell somewhere in between black and white.

every day

Every day my mother waited for me at the bus stop. Her eyes anxious, her mouth ready to smile. Her aura was light, heavenly. She seemed so happy, I didn't want to crush her with stories of my colored confusion. So I lied.

Every day I filled her ears with tales of my popularity and acceptance. I told her that so many girls wanted to play with me at recess that I had to choose. I told her that girls always wanted to share their snacks with me, and that was why I wasn't really hungry at dinner. I told her that one of my classmates invited me to her birthday party this Saturday, but because we were going to Baltimore, I said I couldn't go. I told her that one of the black girls, though I said brown girls for her virgin ears, brushed my hair at recess every day, telling me that it was the most beautiful hair she'd ever seen.

And I learned that mothers and white people were gullible enough to be fooled by a good story and a smile.

in the dark

For years I watched him sit in his study, enveloped in darkness and immersed in the sound of the guitar spewing blues through speakers perched on either side of his chair. My mother always told him that he would go deaf the way he blasted that music. He told her there was nothing he needed to hear anyway, so what difference did it make. When he said that, her face would crumble, but he wouldn't see that because his eyes had already returned to his glass.

In the dark, he would swirl the amber fluid he called Pop-pop, watching as the liquid ate away at the ice cubes floating on top. His forlorn face reflected emotions that came and went like speeding comets. Gloom. Surprise. Glee. Awe. It was as if his soul were flicking through stations with a remote control, and his face was struggling to catch up. But there was no television. The only sound was the occasional clink of the vanishing ice cubes and crackle of the wax as the pain ripped through the guts of the blues singer wailing away into oblivion.

"The only one that loves me is my mother, and she might be jiving too . . ." Bluesman belted.

The sound of my father's laughter at that one line was like shattering plates. He roared, slapping his knee and throwing back his

9

head at a punch line that eluded me. But just as soon as the laughter began, it ended, and in its stead came salty rivers, forging a path down his face.

In the dark, music played on and on until the moon fell, awaiting the sky's daytime angel. Before it would hit, my mother would descend the stairs to find him sprawled across the floor. She'd scrape him up and half-lead, half-carry him up the stairs to their bedroom where he would plunge into sleep's abyss for two or three hours before leaving the darkness behind for the light of day.

she

He said in the darkness, "Liddy was beautiful, soft, affectionate, unlike them.

Her voice was easy, gentle, not demanding or prying, unlike theirs.

She took me in and let me fill her up with my dreams, goals, love, and desires, unlike them.

She had a face that was always ready to smile and a mouth that was ready to pour forth words of kindness, unlike them.

When she looked at me, me, James Washington, she saw only good things, hope, everything I could be, unlike them.

But I never could be anything that she expected or needed because despite her softness, easiness, openness, and encouragement, the world wouldn't let me forget that I'm black."

and they said

Into the bathroom, the black girls came.
"Hi, Shanna," one said, sneering my name.
"Shanna, we don't like you. You think you're cute.
"Don't look surprised, honey, we've got proof.
"Remember the bus rides all those years in the past.
"You were too good to speak on the bus and in class.
"You always looked down your nose at us.
"I didn't say anything, didn't want to cause a fuss.
"But, you zebra bitch, your cozy days are through.
"We'll make these school days a living hell for you."
With those final words came a slap across my face.
And they taught me that among them I had no place.

almost every day

The fingers. They pinch.
The mouths. They spit.
The feet. They kick.
The hands. They hit.
The fists. They punch.
The teeth. They crunch.
The hands. They shove.
The mouths. They munch.
The feet. They smoosh.
The hands. They push.
The shoes. They squoosh.
The doors. They smush.

And they almost never leave a mark.

mr. and mrs. washington

In quiet moments, the two of them would nestle together in the sunroom, and life was beautiful. She would press her body so closely into his that it seemed that she wanted to meld the two of them into one being. His arm would rest protectively around her, and he might drop grapes or cherries, whatever fruit was in season, into her mouth. As she nibbled, she'd stroke his arm gingerly, tracing a vein across his muscled forearm. He'd lean in, saying something in her ear, and she'd burst out laughing her bell-like laugh.

When they were like that, their thick love pouring through the Mt. Airy house, it was easy to see how I came to be. It was easy to feel like I belonged somewhere. Finally and again. But in those other times, when their love was transparent and thin like a spider's web, I felt like the wind that threatened their survival.

And I hated that feeling.

as the years passed

As the years passed, loneliness became my friend, and I wrapped it around myself because it felt familiar, thus secure. While my peers laughed with each other at lunch, I amused myself. While they confided secrets in each other behind cupped hands, I poured my secrets into my own heart. The loneliness hurt, but it was all I had. I could complain to no one. I swallowed down bile that was meant to be puked up, and in my tan body, the pain was buried.

One day, I promised myself that I would rip away at the flesh that trapped my pain, and when my skin was shredded, the hurt would leave, floating up, and out, and away. The pain would leave, and I'd be able to breathe. Finally.

Those were the thoughts that I embraced in my young, child's body. But as the years passed, I learned that ripping away at the skin just leaves your flesh bruised, and relief rarely comes.

the words

I tried to tell, but the words got stuck in my throat. And when they were dislodged, they came out all wrong.

The three of us were sitting in the sunroom. Dad, Mom, and me. Black, white, and between. I think I was around eight years old, but my soul felt so much older. I was weary from years of un-cried tears.

I looked from mother to father, noting all of their differences. Her softness, his hardness. Her pleasantness, his sternness. Her hope, his anger. Her optimism, his pessimism. I decided to shoot straight down the middle, making my words plain.

"I don't like my school," I said, holding my breath.

My mother looked up from her book. My father didn't look up at all.

"Honey, why not?" she asked, her light voice incompatible with the heaviness in my heart.

I inhaled deeply through clenched teeth, gathering strength before saying, "Nobody likes me."

"Of course, they do. They're always sharing their snacks with you and inviting you places."

Before I could fix my lips around the words, the dam broke, and my face was flooded with tears that raced down my face and toward my heart.

My mother rushed over to me, scooping me into her arms, holding me so close that between my snot and her sweater, I felt that I would suffocate.

I heard my father's voice demand, "Is somebody messing with you?"

"Shh," my mother snapped. "Unlike boys, girls don't cry only if someone is hitting them. You should know that by now."

"Well, why is she crying?"

"I don't know," she said, rocking me. "She probably had a bad day."

I heard my father mumble something. Then I heard his heavy feet walk across the sunroom and go into the house. While my ears were filled with my mother's humming, my heart's grief refused to subside.

the drive

We pulled out of our street and headed toward Wissahickon Avenue. As we waited for the light to turn green, I turned to look at my mother. I smiled at her, and she tweaked my nose before guiding our Volvo station wagon onto Lincoln Drive, which was known for its hairpin turns. The car eased into traffic, which stopped at the Rittenhouse Street light. Joggers and bikers trotted and pedaled across the street in front of cars before making their way onto the path that lined this artery of the Schuylkill River. My eyes followed them down the scenic path, and the scene seemed impossibly perfect. Our car slid into action, challenging the bikers to a race, and as the car accelerated, bursts of color punctuating the serene greenery whirred past. I waved shyly at the helmeted father chauffeuring his helmeted daughter on the path, and he waved back. I was on the edge of wondering why my father never guided me on a pedaled tour when my mother broke into my thoughts, swooping in like a protective momma bird ready to feed her hungry, openmouthed chick.

"You're going to love this restaurant, Shanna. I used to come here with my mother and my sister on girls' day out. We had so much fun drinking tea and eating petits fours. It's one of my favorite memories, and I want to share it with you, my own daughter. By the way, you, my dear, look quite the little lady."

I smiled at her corny British accent, and I reached up to touch the flowers on the front of my hat.

"Hydrangeas are my favorite flowers," my mother had gushed when she saw me eyeing the hat in Sasha's Chapeaux last weekend. "They're like chameleons, the way they change colors every few weeks. The pH levels in the soil make them all different shades, but I prefer to think of them as women hungry for a change of clothes."

She had smoothed down my halo of hair and fitted the hat neatly onto my head. Then she chuckled before saying, "Your dad calls hats lids, and I say that this will top off any outfit."

We had milled around the store for another hour, and I soaked in her musings on hydrangeas. That's how she was. She could drag a tale out forever. This habit annoyed my father, who was quick and direct. I, on the other hand, was enchanted. To me, her lingering stories were like powdered sugar being sprinkled across a pound cake from Denise's Delicacies. Every moment with her was like the dense, sweet mound, and her words were the sugary extra.

"The hydrangeas that my mother grew always started off sky blue. It was the sweetest, most tender shade. A few weeks later, the petals got a whisper of pink. Then a few weeks after that, they were a rich crimson color. That was the color I was waiting for before I agreed to marry your father. Once they turned that shade, I clipped a fistful of them, wrapped them in some ribbon, and drove down Lancaster Avenue, across City Avenue, through West Philly, and into North Philly where I picked him up near that open-air theater at 33rd and Dauphin, the Robin Hood Dell East. We drove to city hall where we were married by Mayor Rizzo. Then, we drove down to Cape May for a week. I called my parents from there and told them the good news."

Suddenly her eyes had glazed over as she concluded her story.

"The next time I went to my parents' house, the hydrangeas were a sad, sad shade of purple. I call it heartbreak purple. That's how they look in their last phase. You always know that death is right around the corner for them, and then winter comes to seal their fate. I hate that purple. That's the color they were the last time I saw my father alive."

She paid for my hat without buying anything for herself, and we walked in silence to the car.

Now, she chattered happily as we cruised along Lincoln Drive and headed for City Avenue, the street that divided Philadelphia from affluent Montgomery County. The same street she had crossed all those years ago when it was still called City Line Avenue. As we glided up City Avenue, the sights swished past. I later came to recognize them as TGI Friday's, where many of the 76ers hang out; Lord & Taylor, where my father worked as a stock boy when he first saw my mother; Saks Fifth Avenue, where a high-profile football player was kicked out for having sex in the ladies fitting room with a young clerk; WDAS, where disc jockeys with thunderous voices that reminded me simultaneously of God and Satan performed their magic; St. Joe's University, where white students existed in a bubble that provided them protection from the decaying black community around it; and the Executive House Luxury Apartments, where a television news anchor kept his girlfriend in the penthouse and his wife on the floor below.

We turned right at the seminary onto Lancaster Avenue and entered a different world. The mansions that greeted us from the side of the road were supposed to be subtle and unassuming, but they came crashing in on my sensibilities. Sure, we had large homes in West Mt. Airy, but because of the sidewalks that bordered each street, the houses seemed friendly, open, and accessible. These houses, with their majestic columns, or expansive, manicured lawns, or rigid topiaries, or winding driveways, or eyeless statues, or some other defining feature, placed a distinct barrier between us and them. They seemed to hold their inhabitants at arm's length, allowing them to reside there, but never to live there, and only if they promised to behave.

I got shivers looking at the houses, and my mother met my apprehension with her calm sureness. "The people on the Main Line are friendlier than these castles they've built. The castles are just walls." She didn't explain further, but I accepted her word as golden, for she had lived there, among them.

We made a right on an unmarked street and pulled into the driveway that led to a pink and white Victorian mansion with a simple sign that read La Fourchette Bed and Breakfast. We rounded the building, and my mother guided the car into a lot filled with luxury cars that sparkled like braced teeth.

She led me up the path without looking, absently stroking her blond hair, which was pulled into a tight ponytail. Looking at her, I noticed for the first time that she was wearing makeup and gold jewelry, and she was carrying a purse that I had never seen. It was harder than the soft, colorful bags she usually carried. Her whole look was harder, as if she were suited up in armor.

Once inside, we went into a room that was as pink as the inside of a clamshell and almost as smothering with its tedious decorations. We sat at a small pink table near the window in the dining room of the bed and breakfast, and I felt the need to hold my breath because any large movement threatened to break everything in the room, including the delicate pink women holding their delicate pink teacups. Napkin placed on her lap and smile plastered on her face, my mother was transformed into a Main Line maven, speaking in modest tones and nodding politely and waving at familiar tan faces not dissimilar from her own. She blended in perfectly while I stuck out like a fly in buttermilk. The lump in my throat wouldn't allow me to swallow the ornately dressed food, and as I looked around the pink room, I saw the women as walls, set in place to maintain a façade that I didn't understand. I caught my mother's eye, and sadness washed over her face.

"I'm sorry," she whispered with her head down as she removed some bills from her purse. She removed her gold earrings and placed them on the table as she collected her things and hurried from the dining room and into the foyer.

"That's a heck of a tip," I said, smiling and taking off my hat.

"Yeah. They're old, from my past, and the past has a way of weighing you down."

We ambled back to the car and drove happily back home.

falling down

We were at Miles Park for a picnic on Memorial Day. I remember it like it was yesterday because it marked the onset of a series of changes in my life. I should have known that the picnic was just the beginning of imminent change because bad things always happen in threes.

Mom, determined to bring us closer as a family, had packed a picnic basket of delectable delicacies. Shrimp salad on fat, crusty bagels from Rosensweig's Deli. Corn and tomato salsa to cover gourmet chicken burritos from Don Pepe's. Sweet Potato French Fries and Surprise Iced Tea from Sugarene's Soul Food Spot.

Dad had laid out the blanket and was beginning a game of solitaire while Mom pulled out the latest Danielle Steel book. I pulled out my jump rope and attempted to jump rope on a flat patch of grass.

Conversation was always sparse in our household, and I was used to it, but sometimes under my father's watchful, wordless stare I grew uncomfortable. It seemed that in his watching, he was waiting. Waiting. Ever waiting for me to make a mistake. Mess up. And when I did, he would pounce.

"Watch what you're doing!"

"You're making a mess!"

"Look at yourself! You're such a slob."

"Damn it! Can't you do anything right?"

So I tried to be perfect. Maybe in my perfection, I could gain his acceptance. That Memorial Day, I gained more than acceptance. I gained his love. At least temporarily.

Tired of jumping rope, I went to explore the Kiddie Community. There were minihouses like sheds, complete with flower boxes and benches. Not interested in the frilly girl's stuff inside, I peered up to the roof. Boys on other roofs walked their big-stepped walk, happy and free. The sun beat down on their faces, and under its warm glare, their colors melted into one. They were all golden brown in its rays. I wanted to be up there. In the sun. In with the others. Like the others.

So I climbed up and up like Jack and the Beanstalk until I reached the top. It wasn't that high, only about seven feet, but on top, I felt like the queen of the world. I tried to do the big-stepped walk, claiming every inch between my feet, on top of the roof, in the world. I wanted to be big, complete, perfect, but in my quest for perfection I stumbled, and I, like Icarus, came crashing to the earth. The sun, my betrayer, beat down on me.

From outside of my body, I watched my father spring into action. He scooped me up and carried me to the car. Alone, just the two of us, he charged down Germantown Pike, racing for my life. Through stoplights he sped, pressing his shirt under my chin, trying to stop the bleeding. There in the car, through the fear, through the worry, through the pain, I saw that the way to his heart was through danger. As long as my physical needs were met, he didn't worry. Yet if I were in harm's way, he would save me.

?

Why did my mother leave her monied Main Line home?

Was the love that she had for my father the only lure?

Was she purposely leaving something behind?

Why hadn't she ever gone back?

Was there a wall that kept her out of her home, or was it a self-imposed exile?

Why hadn't she taken me there to claim my roots and take my place at the table?

Why didn't any of her old friends come to visit us?

Had she purposely kept them away?

Had she ever wanted to go back?

Had she ever wanted to forget about us and fade back into her old environment seamlessly with tales of some exotic safari or an extended stay in some quaint European village?

Why did she cry sometimes when she thought I was sleeping or playing?

Was she longing to go back, or did she have newer, fresher wounds that drove crystal-like tears to her eyes?

Did she feel trapped in a world in which she didn't completely fit?

Was my father her jailer?

Was I?

When she laughed with her new friends was it real laughter, or was it a mask?

Did she feel like she was serving a sentence complete with hard labor?

Did she mind cooking, cleaning, and picking up after us even though she wasn't raised for the drudgery of middle-class life?

Did she have other dreams?

Had she loved before my father?

What happened to her parents?

When and where did her relief come?

thing two of three

I turned nine that summer, and I had my first real birthday party complete with decorations and a cake. My dad had broken his rule about staying out of North Philly, and he had checked his disgust and gone to Denise's Delicacies for my cake.

"They have the best cakes in the city," my mother had whined.

My father's jaw had been tight as he clenched his teeth and looked at me. I scratched at the scar on my chin, and I could see guilt dance in his eyes before he snapped at me.

"Leave your face alone!"

Mumbling, he collected his keys and headed back to the place from which he hailed, the place he'd grown to despise.

"Mommy, why does he hate going to North Philly?" I questioned after hearing his car pull away.

She sighed and wiped her hands on her apron, wondering what to say and how to say it.

"Your dad had a hard childhood," she began, wondering where to tread and what to reveal.

My innocent eyes compelled her to continue speaking.

"I don't really know how to explain it because I'm not sure if I fully understand it myself. He just got tired of life there."

"Why?"

"I don't know, honey. But he hates everything that reminds him of there, and he loves anything that's different," she said.

Then I heard her sniffle before her head went down. She wept silently while fingering her wedding band.

That afternoon, my mother's family, which consisted of her mother, her younger sister, and her older brother, poured into our home to celebrate my birthday. My mom dished up the cake while my dad served drinks. He kept his glass filled, and every time he got the chance, he refilled the glass of my mom's younger sister. She smiled appreciatively and soon she began giggling whenever he approached. Soon, the two of them disappeared. Together.

imitation of life

My mother said, "This has always been one of my favorite movies."

I sat next to her, popcorn in hand, taking in the opening credits while watching the growing cluster of diamonds at the bottom of the TV screen. My mother's eyes glazed over. I didn't know it then, but she was remembering her old life. Equestrian lessons, lavish dinners, and white gloves had all been a part of her upbringing. As Lana Turner floated about the set in fabulous clothes, my mother wondered, just for a split second, why she had walked away. I didn't know it then, so no fear of rejection clamped my mouth quiet, forcing me to be still for fear of being thrown away.

So I jostled.

I fidgeted.

I squirmed.

My attention couldn't be stilled for the moment, so I got up and went into the dining room to play with the colored paper a neighbor had given me for origami. A little while later I heard stifled sounds, and I poked my head back into the living room. My mother was still sitting in the same place on the couch, but her head was down. Her shoulders shook spasmodically, and muffled words and gasps squeaked out of her throat intermittently.

"Mommy, I'm so sorry I left you. I'm so sorry."

Her soft voice was swallowed up by Mahalia Jackson's fuller one. Mahalia's burden-bearing grief was so common that it seemed almost rehearsed. She and other black women were used to hurting, and they displayed their despair openly, readily. And the world would know their history and their present, so they would let them weep. But as my mother wept, her voice small, her reasons obscured by race and circumstance, I wondered who sings the white woman's blues.

rememory

He was slow in starting his music, but quick in pouring the Old Grand-Dad that day. And as he settled in his chair between the two soundless speakers, he began his rememory. I watched him from the dining room where I sat under the table folding black construction paper into a swan. As the first words passed from his lips, I felt guilty, like I was eavesdropping on a confession.

Then he spoke.

"Hip-dip Gibson was a funny cat. Boy, he could hold some juice. You never even knew he was drinkin' 'til he started to laugh. Laughed real high when he was tastin'. Like a girl. Like a little girl gigglin' at a joke her best friend told her. Yeah, that was Hip-dip. And when he was gigglin', Chicken Wilson would start in.

"Chicken Wilson always carried a wishbone in his shirt pocket. The other men razzed him about that wishbone because it was a new one every day. Pork used to ask him if his country ass had just finished eating some Southern-fried yard bird. Chicken Wilson would pick his teeth with the toothpick he always sucked, and he would say, 'I'd tell you what I just finished eating, but your ol' lady might get mad at me for tellin'.' Hip-dip would go fallin' out. So would Pork and Chicken himself. The only one who wouldn't laugh outright was Sarge. He would just do a sly side-smile, like this here . . .'"

My father smiled to himself, his lips forming a sideways isosceles triangle before taking another gulp of Pop-pop.

"Yeah, he would sneak a smile and say, 'Not in front of the boy.' He'd nod in my direction. They'd get sober, straight serious like they were his troops. He'd put 'em at ease again, though. Say somethin' like, 'I don't know why a yard bird would waste his time arguing with swine anyway. Swine got a forked hoof and a forked tongue, split right down the middle. They never know what direction they goin'.

"Only person who could talk like that to Chicken Wilson, Pork, and Hip-dip Gibson was Sarge. Respect. That's what he commanded. Respect."

And as my father moved to turn on Art Blakey and the Jazz Messengers, he mumbled, "Sarge was the last born man."

Then music overtook him, and he sank into the chair, Pop-pop licking at the ice specks in his glass.

cream

My mother called it crème brûlée. My father called it high yellow. Whatever you call it, it's my skin, my wrapping, my shell, and it's all I've got. The truth is, I've never hated it. It just always seemed to cause confusion for other people.

"What do you consider yourself?"

"What kind of man will you marry?"

"You listen to rap?"

"Well, at least your butt's not flat."

"Are your boobies pink or brown?"

"Can you sing?"

"I bet you've got rhythm."

"I bet y'all are rich."

"Are you, like, poor?"

"Y'all eat soul food?"

"Do you guys, like, eat that weird stuff?"

"You're so exotic looking."

"What's up redbone?"

"What do you consider yourself?"

Those people broke through my racial oblivion, grasped at the lies circling about in their heads, smashed them all together, tied them up in a ribbon, and handed the confusion back to me like it was a gift. What was I supposed to do with that? They thought I was supposed to be confused, tragic, and conflicted. They thrust it upon me, so now maybe I am.

This cream wrapping I'm in has a smoothness that belies the storm beneath. A poet wrote of the flea that contained the blood of two warring enemies. But they were in love. That man and that woman were supposed to remain separate. They were supposed to be sworn enemies. But the flea bit one, then the other, and big surprise, it didn't die from the mingling of their blood. So the man spent a considerable amount of time kicking game to her, trying to convince her to come over to his side. She couldn't possibly exist there, and he couldn't possibly live in her world, so they had to meet in the middle.

In a place like Mt. Airy, I'm their flea. I couldn't reside in his ghetto or her utopia, so I'm stuck in between. And there is a war raging under my cream skin. One general tells me to be angry, to lash out, to fight the power. The other tries to pacify me, attempting to get me to quash the rage. I'm not sure which way to go.

And it terrifies me.

then

My father sat in the living room, glass in hand, remembering the old words as if they had been carved on his heart.

"He said to me, 'Son, your mother wasn't always as hard as she is now. I know you don't believe that, but it's true. She was always slow to smile, though. First, she'd act like you weren't there. Walk right past like you didn't exist. Then, she'd act like you were in her way, underfoot like. Then, she'd pretend that since you were there, you might as well give her a hand with something. Earn your keep. Then, she acts like you were supposed to be there, like it was some sort of unspoken agreement. Then, she'd study you real careful-like to make sure you were real and that she could expect you and depend on you to be there. Then, and only then, would she twist her mouth sideways and crack her lips just a little. Her mouth would light up her whole face, and it felt like summertime.'"

thing three of three

My mother was gone. She left us at the end of the summer. Just walked away leaving a note for my father in her stead.

> James,
>
> I should have known. I should have known that you could never love me when you hate yourself. I thought I could help heal you. Lift you up. Lead you to love. I lit the path, but you wouldn't follow.
>
> Know that I don't hate you. I don't hate my sister. I don't hate any of the others. I don't hate my child. Please make sure she knows that. I just need to preserve myself since no one else will.
>
> I love you. Tell Shanna that I love her with all of my heart, but I have to go. Please love her. Love her more than you've loved me. Let her know that the skin she's in is not a curse. Make her know that she has a place between black and white.
>
> Elizabeth

He folded up her letter and put it in a drawer. He never mentioned her again.

the four fathers

They sat on milk crates a few yards back from the corner of 18th and Erie in North Philly. The corner itself was busy, and the black belt bustle would distract them, keeping them locked in the swish of the present as opposed to the comfort of the yesterday they missed and the hope of the tomorrow they longed for. They were the four fathers of James' youth.

Their skins varied in color from Hip-dip Gibson's high yellow to Sarge's sable. Their pasts varied, too, from Pork's past life as a butcher to Chicken Wilson's former existence as a history instructor at the black men's college just south of Philadelphia. Their current paths mingled, swirling, incorporating Sarge's fatigue green with Pork's blood red and Hip-dip's uptown blues with Chicken Wilson's high-collared starched white until what remained was a kaleidoscope of colors. Some thought the kaleidoscope was an ugly mess, so they averted their eyes when walking past in an effort not to see the patchwork colors and the patchwork men. But to James the colors were a soft, inviting rainbow. The colors were shades that didn't ex- ist inside of the dreary apartment of James' youth. There, only in- stitutional pea green lived. The deep-voiced sounds, too, were missing from his smothering cave, but like an itch that had gone unscratched for so long that the body forgot its unfulfilled discomfort, the voices settled into James' ears, releasing a pleasure-filled "Ahhh" of satisfaction.

Some of the neighborhood ladies sucked their teeth in passing, clucking their tongues and muttering about how it wasn't decent for the four men to sit idly around on the street. It was Pork who wanted to fuss back every time the assault came, but Sarge shushed him, never raising his eyes from cleaning his nails. Sarge knew that if anybody had earned the right to sit pat, resting their weary bones and aching backs, it was old black men.

Keeping a lid on their power, forcing it to lie dormant all of those years, had been exhausting work. White men feared the power. White women fueled it. Black women fought it. So the only thing for them to do so that they could stay safe was to stuff it back down as if it never existed. To others, it appeared to be laziness, but the four, they knew. And they acknowledged each other's manhood.

James was an extension of their manhood. He was the only one they didn't shoo away when he lingered on his way home from school or to the corner store. He needed their history, and they needed his hope. It was a relationship beneficial to all involved. Chicken Wilson dropped history on him, Pork schooled him in community economics, Hip-dip Gibson enlightened him about the art of cultural refinement, and Sarge demonstrated personal responsibility and dignified manhood. They were his street corner fathers, and he needed them desperately to complete the equation of his being. They needed him, for he was a star that traveled alone on a course. If he burned too brightly, someone might snuff his light out, but if his light were too dim, no one would ever see his beauty. They taught him to moderate himself, to stay the course, and to flare up when the time was right. They were his fathers, and he loved them.

how

I remember wondering...

...how can I face the dawn each day without her gentle voice nudging me into consciousness?

...how can I look into my closet at the rows of neatly ironed clothes, knowing that her hands, which had smoothed the wrinkled fabric into submission, weren't ever going to do that again?

...how can I descend the stairs as usual when the breakfast that she used to make with care would not await me in the kitchen?

...how can I make my way to the bus without my guardian angel there to guide me?

...how can I make it through the day with all of my school secrets stuffed down inside of me with no one to tell?

...how can I get off the bus and head home without her hopeful eyes making me feel some semblance of security?

...how can I return to a house that is quiet, save for the occasional blaring sound of empty music. Just sounds, no words?

But most of all, I remember wondering, how can a mother just leave her child?

good hair

They always told me that I had good hair. The black girls. They, who spent Saturday mornings trapped in hot kitchens with frustrated mothers yanking their heads to and fro while putting three-hundred-degree steel combs so close to their daughters' scalps that the popping beads of sweat sizzled, burning them, envied me. They, whose eyes watered and fingers throbbed as they clenched their teeth and fists and counted forward, backward, and forward again before their jaws began to clench shut as the relaxer burned through the epidermis of their scalps, envied me. They, whose big sisters pinned them between steel traps called knees on the front steps while pulling at the roots of hair that seemed to be affixed to brain matter and who had instant face-lifts every weekend, envied me.

"You've got good hair," one might murmur as she gazed on my tresses with eyes pulled open so tightly that I wondered if she slept like a fish.

Good hair.

She didn't know any better. Science told of dominant and recessive genes, but I landed smack in the middle of it all.

My father's hair, with its dark curls so tight that they formed multidimensional circles that looked like the letter O, had combined with my mother's hair, straight like vermicelli and bright like sunshine. The results were my amber-colored locks whose long, relaxed curls fell in thick, snaky cascades as beautifully dangerous as Victoria Falls. Beautiful because the curls formed wisps reminiscent of the winding mists rising up from the rushing falls. Dangerous because they, like I, didn't know that they were supposed to stay down, didn't know where they belonged, and like a cornered animal that might lash out from fear, I, too, had the potential to strangle out of fear. I didn't know it then. Neither did the little girls envious of me and my carefree curls. They only saw the semblance of beauty in my cream skin and good hair. They never saw the confused danger lurking beneath.

the knowing

It didn't take long for James to realize which one was his father because the knowing always begins in the soul.

The one who shushed the others when vulgarity peppered their stories.

The one who always slipped him an extra four dollars at the end of each week, saying simply, "Here's something for your pocket."

The one who stared into James' eyes with intensity, hanging on to his every word when asked about how he was doing with his lessons.

The one who took him to Mr. Silk's on Market Street to find him a tie to wear for graduation.

The one who taught him how to shake hands firmly with a manly grip.

The one who told him to look a person in the eye, and smile from time to time because that's the way to gain trust.

James thought that the final lesson could have been best kept a secret because it hadn't made his mother trust that man at all.

James' street corner father said, "I learned that lesson too late in life, so she never believed me when I said I loved her. I did, though. I still do."

And James knew that, too.

black boyhood

He had known that he had to wear the armor when he ventured out of his community. Segregation had provided him asylum, a refuge in which he was free to chase girls with a stick he'd used to scrape a dead bird down the "souwee" hole, as they called it. He had been free to shout as loudly as his lungs would permit as he and his friends played stickball in the street. He had been free to take his time ordering candy at Slim Jim's corner store because Slim wasn't going to snap at him, attributing his indecisiveness to inferiority. It was only when he was scrubbed free of the familiar and comfortable dirt, greased down in the oppressive petroleum jelly, and trapped in the suffocating starched clothing that he knew he had to put his game face on.

"Act dignified," his mother hissed as she yanked him down the steps of the apartment, guiding him past the four fathers on the milk crates, down Erie Avenue to Broad Street where they took the bus downtown.

They sat quietly, eyes straight ahead, heading toward the uncertainty of Center City, praying to be spared of the indignities that threatened to topple even the most outwardly assured-looking black person. When they returned home, if there had been no humiliation, no slights, no ignominy, her good mood would inspire her to cut him an extra large piece of cake or give him an extra scoop of butter pecan ice cream.

But there were those other times. Those other times when she felt the shame of being a single mother without the benefit of loving black arms there to hold her. Those other times when she felt the sting of never having been protected by any black man since that no good daddy of hers went and got himself killed when she was a child in Virginia. Those other times when she felt the smack of loneliness, poverty, and ugly white hate all at once. And she would look into the big, beautiful eyes of her son, gaze upon his sweet dark chocolate skin, and regard his tender little hands still dented over the knuckles like a baby's. And she wanted to break him hard and clean before the world would have the chance to. Cut him to the quick before he'd ever know that she was imperfect and unable to protect him. Snap him to the bone before he got any big ideas that the world would steal before stilling him in dejection.

And while he knew that he needed to shield himself from the outside world, he never guessed that emotional danger could present itself within the pea green walls of his home. So he was unprepared for the sting of the words the first time he heard them.

"You no good, black-ass nigger. You'll grow up to be just like the rest of 'em. Worthless like a pile of shit."

They had stunned him, shaken him, stopped him from breathing. Her face, so beautiful, had just opened, revealing a gory, fleshy mass of ugliness. He had tripped trying to hurry away from her, rushing down the steps and out to the four fathers. Hip-dip had given him a peppermint for his stomach. Chicken Wilson had given him a quarter for his pocket. Pork had given him a kerchief for his face. Sarge had given him silence. He knew the roots of James' tears, but he didn't know what to tell him to stop the hurt. The truth is, she had hurt him, too, but no one, observing from the outside, would believe that. From the outside she had every right to be bitter, having to raise a child seemingly without the help of his father. But they would never know that she ran him away with her barbed words. Now she was running her son away. With every foul utterance, she would push him further and further away until he would never return. Until he would only respond to the kindness of white women. Until he would produce a half-black, half-white daughter who would try to piece together her past, present, and future in her own solitary world because he was too afraid to help her.

why

As I grew older, I began to understand my father's roots. And I began to know his pain. And I began to see how his mother had defrauded him of real love and a real chance at happiness. And I began to see how his anger at her could shape his attitude toward other women, me included. And I began to see how it could seep out at the seams. And I began to see that my father was a victim. And I began to see how, in this inferior stance, he would strike out at his wife, who epitomized what he and many others perceived as superior.

And even though I understood all of the elements that added up to the picture that is my dad, and even though I understood that the marriage was dysfunctional at best, and even though I often didn't feel like I belonged there, I can't understand why my mother would leave me.

And I can't help thinking that maybe I was what she was running away from.

part two

black

my sanctuary

My apartment is in the section of North Philly that whites have carved out for themselves. They call it Northern Liberties, and like other gentrified enclaves around the city, it can be described as quaint. With its urban gardens, balconied apartments, and upscale eateries, some might even call it chic. I see it for what it is, though. It's a whitewashed front. It's brickface on a hovel. It's a freshly bathed whore, and if scratched too deeply, it's bound to reveal its ugliness. So the people of Northern Liberties don't scratch. They coexist peacefully, trying to keep their backs from getting pressed to the wall so that they never utter the N-word. But if pressed, they simply move out, returning to their homogeneous comfort zones because they have somewhere else they can go. So do I, even though I'd hate to do so. Even as I sit here in my own sanctuary, I know that I am a farce. A fucking joke.

I'm a nineteen-year-old college student, and when I tell my Temple schoolmates that I live in North Philly, they never pursue it further. I'm glad that they don't because then I'd have to reveal that I reside in Northern Liberties, and they'd say that I'm not really down. Like an ugly fat girl working as a phone sex operator. They'd view me like the Oreo that I am, and I couldn't stand that again. The truth is, I'm only fooling myself. Where else in this section of the city could I park a doorless Wrangler? Nowhere but in the gated compound of Liberty Square. Where else in this section of the city could I return safely from a campus party at two o'clock in the morning? Where else could I create a refuge in the heart of the chaos in my mind and the chaos of this community?

My apartment is a two-bedroom deal on the second floor. It's white and maple throughout, creating a conflicting sense of warm sterility. Furniture is sparse, as my needs are few. My maple kitchen table doubles as a packing area for my photography jobs. One of the bedrooms is my darkroom, and the other is where I sleep and study. My futon there faces a large picture window that I rarely open. I prefer artificial light in this bedroom, so I have track lights arranged in a square on my ceiling. All of them point in varying directions, throwing light everywhere. One row is different, though.

The lights on this row are aimed at an eight-by-eight canvas that's spread on a wooden frame that hangs on the wall behind my futon. The canvas displays a black-and-white photo that I took in high school. The photo was taken in the park. I remember the day that I took it like it was yesterday.

It was my sixteenth birthday, and when I got home from school, a package was waiting in the mailbox. It had no return address and no postmark, so I knew that it had been hand-delivered. I opened the brown wrapping paper, and inside was a pair of gold earrings like the ones my mother had left on the table of that restaurant so long ago. She had worn them then as an act of remembrance, and here they sat in a box in my hand, showing me that she hadn't forgotten me. That day, I had cried and smiled and smiled and cried because for years, all I had wanted to know was that my mother remembered me despite her disappearance from my life when I was a child. I needed to document and preserve something that day to make it permanent, so I had walked out of my house and down Wissahickon Avenue toward Lincoln Drive. I had wandered on the walking path that edges the artery of the Schuylkill, and I had sat by the water, looking at the most permanent, unchanging thing I knew. I picked up my camera and aimed the lens at the grove of trees. And I snapped one picture that day because I knew that the one picture would be perfect, that it would be enough. And three years later, it stands on my bedroom wall. Trees, tall and strong with limbs reaching up above the canvas and out to me through time and space. Reminding me of my mother who was distant yet still so close. Like the photograph of the trees, though, she was an illusion, and I hated her for leaving me, at the same time I loved her for providing me with shelter in my early years.

vice

Men are my vice, my weakness, and I allow them to come to me, to fill me because, like a vault that's been plundered, I am so empty.

I don't know when the emptiness began, but I became aware of it when my mother left, and it was magnified during all of those years that I lived alone with my father. Except for his music and his occasional awkward angry words, I went unacknowledged. No "I-love-yous." No "You're-beautifuls." Yet my heart ached to hear those words from him. From anyone. Now I know how to get them to say it.

When they are here, their words take over the silence. They are desperate to have me . . . rather it . . . so they'll say anything that I want to hear. But sometimes their throaty whispers are muffled in the sheets, and I can't hear them. Or sometimes, their words leave me as soon as they leave me, and I must go on a quest to find another speaker. Another lover who will fill me, taking away my emptiness. Another who will make me feel whole. For at least an hour while we dance the dance.

my mother's gift

The jeep had been a high school graduation gift from my mother. It had been parked in the driveway in the middle of the night, and an envelope containing the keys, the title, the insurance card, and the registration had been left in the mailbox. The car was registered in both of our names, but her Main Line address was the only one listed. For the graduation, there had been no congratulatory phone call, no bundle of flowers, nothing in the way of personal touches that conveyed true caring, though, and that was enough to hurt my heart. The tears had formed in my chest, and they had made their way up my throat, readying themselves behind my lids when I saw a second key lodged in the corner of the envelope. A string was looped through the hole, and a small piece of paper was attached to the end. It read simply "Mom," and I knew that it was the key to her home. I toyed with rage and contentment before settling on acceptance. She just wanted me to know that I could get to her if I needed to. But why hadn't she been brave enough to face me, the one she'd abandoned?

the lens

I fell in love with the lens when I was fifteen. In that stage of swirling emotions, I dug the way I could manipulate the lens and create flatness. Flatness of emotion and energy. Yet, if I wished, I could also capture frenzy and excitement. The camera and the lens became my means of control. Despite the circumstances surrounding me, I could create peace. Thinking of it still gives me a rush, and in egomaniacal moments, I imagine, just for a split second, what it's like to be God.

At my high school, I came to be known as somewhat of a beatnik, complete with my weed-smoking and my endless supply of black clothes. I was the Herb Ritts of Girls' High. I was the Photography Club *and* the Art Club. I didn't like taking pictures for the newspaper or the yearbook because the shots were always so staged.

"Here's Becky, the president of Rotary Interact. Smile, Becky."

Click.

"Here's Yolanda, captain of the basketball team. Yolanda, hold up that basketball for us and say cheese."

Click.

Even the ones that were supposed to be candid were fake.

"See the Key Club as they box up the donations from this year's Christmas Drive. Aren't they magnanimous?"

Click.

Everyone has an image they want to convey, a way they want to be seen. Then, there's the truth. That's what I try to capture on film. The truth. But truth, like the temporary love I find, is fleeting and conditional. Yet still I try.

north philly

As soon as I could drive, I found my way from Mt. Airy to North Philly. Call it a study in contrasts, call it a study in personal pedigree, call it thrill seeking. Whatever it was, I wanted to unearth what my father had spent his whole adult life shunning.

Armed with my camera, a bottle of water, and mace, I slid into my Wrangler and ventured from comfort to chaos. As I approached Broad and Erie, tornadoes of trash were whipped about by dry gusts of wind. The smell of ribs being barbequed in half of an oil drum permeated the air. Bursts of music broke forth from cars that looked like they were taped together driven by men who seemed to be held together by string. Young women dressed like call girls and shaped like kidney beans led parades of children into corner stores where dour, yellow-skinned merchants, trained in hearing through thick Plexiglas, glowered at them in disgusted amusement. Stumps of men all garbed in long white T-shirts and dark baggy jeans in a show of solidarity among criminals half-swaggered, half-hopped around in circles on the corner, lobbying for the attention of potential customers and potential lovers. Children with dusty skin and ashy knees shouted round sounds to each other in raspy voices. All of their laughter, pain, frustration, and glee were bandied about for all to see.

They held nothing back. Why should they? They didn't know they were being watched or judged as they raced down the street, untied dirty sneakers carrying them past hot, three-story dens. They had no idea that with my camera out, I could capture them as they were, not as they hoped to be. No "best-foot-forward" dress rehearsal here. Langston Hughes would have been proud. Old ladies, bloated by age and despair, turned their fat heads slowly in my direction as I sat at the corner of Bouvier, watching me watching them. Even after I smiled and waved, they glared on, each set of eyebrows gathered in a vicious V, too untrusting to embrace me as one of their own, yet too vulnerable and helpless to question me. Sure, they'd talk about me after I was gone, but not one would gather the strength to approach me to ask what I thought I was doing taking pictures in their neighborhood.

As I ventured further south, settling momentarily in one enclave then another, I saw ghosts of people emerging from shells of houses that were once prominent districts where black professionals resided. Integration had ushered the muckety-mucks into suburban centers like Laverock, Wyncote, and Glenside, and they had abandoned marble-staired, parquet-floored urban palaces, which were promptly scooped up, subdivided, and rented out to anyone who could dig up a money order. What remained were magnificently structured holding cells from which people spilled forth onto front stoops and sidewalks where they played cards, rolled dice, laughed, and cursed through chipped teeth. With my camera on my lap, I viewed them as broken people without hope or help being sustained by some unknown force. Later I would find out that that unknown force was strength and spirit, but on this day when I raised my camera to my face, the lens was my father's eye, and I saw the people as ghosts who had deserted the body called The Dream. Through the lens, the men became shiftless thugs, waiting for me to turn my back so that they could rob me. Through the lens, the women became egg-holders ready to be fertilized so that they could trap men and keep them caught in the place where people shit on dreams and spit at opportunity. Through the lens, the children became time bombs, waiting to explode and crying for attention that no one gives them. Through the lens, North Philly was a wasteland where the sun didn't shine and flowers didn't grow. But as I was leaving, I thought I heard a pulse.

with racing heart 1

With racing heart
I climbed the tree
To rescue her
Little kitty.
He had climbed up
Now won't come down
People in shock
Gathered around
I held on tight
Fingers in grooves
Inching toward him
He did not move.
Out on the limb,
He looked so scared
I grabbed him fast.
His life was spared.
We moved back toward
The tree's big trunk.
I smelled my a-
drenaline's funk.

Heading toward ground
I felt a high.
Like Icarus,
thought I could fly.
With racing heart,
I climbed that tree
Still aching for him
To rescue me.

him

I've always tried to freeze people in the moment so that their raw purity could be exposed. Those moments just come to me. I can't create them. So I must wait. That's what I was doing the first time I saw him.

He raced into my peripheral vision as I sat on a bench on 12th Street in the heart of Temple University's campus. As I leaned with my back against the table, with my camera resting on my stomach, I felt his heat before I saw him. I fumbled for my camera, but my breath was caught in my chest as I watched the northbound specimen in admiration. His white tank top seemed all too stingy in revealing his glowing bronze skin. His tight shoulders led to arms etched with muscles. His torso was lean, his stomach flat. His behind was tight and high, and his legs, ripped with muscles, carried him quickly as he sprinted away.

Something stayed with me long after he was gone. Though his face looked relaxed, his hands were drawn into tight fists, telling me that his heart was torn. I wanted to get inside of that torn heart to mend it from the inside out. And in the meantime, I was hoping that he could fill the empty silence that was my world.

home

Even though Temple's campus is a thirty-minute drive to Mt. Airy, I don't go home as often as one would expect. I don't feel guilty about it, and my dad seems pretty indifferent as well, so that works fine for me. But every few weeks, I leave my apartment and make the trek north on Broad Street, heading back to the home that hasn't felt like a home since my mother deserted me, saving herself, all those years ago.

I sift through the mail, flick through the cable stations, thumb through magazines, rummage through the fridge, and loll around in the sunroom until he gets home.

My back stiffens when I hear his keys in the door, and I smooth my hair and clothes as I hear the door open. I clear my throat of the angry bile that has built up, and I try to greet him with a bright smile and a light voice.

"Hey, Dad," I say.

"Hi, Shanna," he returns.

I click my mind on autopilot and I chatter away, filling him in on details of my grades, news of visits by leading intellectuals, sports updates, and campus events. He listens attentively, nodding where he should smile and "Mm-hmming" every once in a while.

I ask him about his mother, and he gives a brief summary of her condition.

"... wasting her money on the lottery ... not taking her medicine like she should ... gambling in Atlantic City ... drinking too much ..."

Of all the things he describes, my father and his mother share only one vice, and the irregularity of his indulgence doesn't allow him to see the danger in his bingeing, while he recognizes the risk of hers.

I avert my eyes from his wrist after I see the sparkle of a new bracelet dangling there. It's from Tiffany, and I know that he's too cheap to have bought it for himself. So I know that it's a gift, and I know that it's probably from the redhead whose long strand of hair I found in the bathroom sink. And I know that it's another thing we won't talk about.

We challenge each other in *Jeopardy*, and I beat his ass mercilessly because I hate him for driving my mother away and for all of the words that he could never say, all of the silence that forced me to deliver myself into the arms of men only out to satisfy their lust while I try to mend my soul. Afterward, he looks at me in awe. Then we watch *The Simpsons*, and we share laughter at Bart's antics because while I hate my father, I also love him because he took care of me after my mother abandoned me. Afterward, he looks at me with love. But he doesn't say anything.

Soon I get up and head out to my jeep, muttering excuses about needing to get back to my apartment to write a paper. He nods as I leave, unspoken words still lingering on his lips.

I decide to take the long way back to campus, and I peel out of the driveway, heading toward Lincoln Drive, which will lead me to Kelly Drive, the curvy extension of Lincoln Drive. Seat belt undone, I whip around the snaky path that flanks the Schuylkill River. With racing heart, I navigate its womanly curves, and scream my pain with Teena Marie, a kindred soul searching for a home. Then I think of my mother, wondering why he tried to steal her life when all she tried to do was breathe life into him. And I wonder just who the victim is.

one o'clock

I determined that with his runner's physique, he was a creature of habit. That habit would lead him back to 12th Street where he would run north like his ancestors had probably done generations before. He would pass briefly through my life again at one o'clock. I sat ready, like a cheetah waiting to pounce, camera ready to capture his naked edge.

Again I felt his heat before I saw him. I wondered what it was about him that made me sense his presence. It was like I was a heat-seeking missile, and he was my target, only that analogy made me feel too predatory. Whatever it was, I was drawn toward him, and I hoped that the camera's eye would catch and preserve it until I could catch him.

I lifted the camera to my eye and pointed it in his direction, moving slowly to match his pace as he approached.

Click.

Calm.

Click.

Ease.

Click.

Despair.

Click.

Peace.

Click.

Pleasure.

Click.

Pain.

Click.

Happiness.

Click.

A nod and a smile at me.

Click.

Got him.

north philly: take two

I was in search of Jill Scott's North Philly, so I went exploring again. This time I set out on foot. In Timbs, cargo pants, and a white T-shirt with my backpack filled with my water and a camera strapped to my shoulders, I wandered north on Broad first, toward Susquehanna, past the dollar store, nail shop, hair salon, check-cashing place, and Chinese food store. Like a vagrant, I meandered aimlessly, and with each step I blew dust off of the unrecognized gem that was North Philly.

I saw the Uptown Theater that had hosted black performers when other venues in the city had turned them away. Old neighborhood griots were happy to recount stories to me of brown people in all of their finery converging on the hall, clutching their four-dollar admission tickets tightly so that they could see Pookie Hudson and the Spaniels, Jerry Butler, Harold Melvin and the Blue Notes, and the Motown Revue.

I saw Girard College, a boarding school for fatherless boys whose founder had made a gentleman's agreement barring the admission of black boys. As I walked, old brown men proudly revealed tales of hoisting young brown men over the campus wall in a forceful show of integration.

I saw the home of Jessie Redmon Fauset, the Harlem Renaissance heroine who, as the literary editor of the NAACP's *Crisis* magazine, published the works of Langston Hughes and others for the first time. Fauset, a graduate of my high school, Girls' High, had been a quiet launching force for one of America's greatest literary eras.

I saw the Divine Lorraine Hotel, one of the city's old black hotels, which had been founded by a Garvey-like minister named Father Divine. He was called controversial by white media, but blacks knew that the only controversy centered around his call for black financial independence.

I saw Cecil B. Moore Avenue, named after the civil rights lawyer and activist who, in his characteristic kick-ass manner served as the voice of Philadelphia's black community during the 1950s and '60s. As a city councilman and president of the local branch of the NAACP, he lobbied for blacks to get jobs paying respectable wages. An old man, who was sitting on his steps doing crossword puzzles and chewing on a toothpick, was proud to tell me that his cousin Buster had been hired as a bricklayer to help construct Strawberry Mansion High School as a result of old Cecil B.

North Philly was brimming with riches, but like the downtown New Yorkers who were living on top of the African burial grounds, the residents didn't know it. With my camera in hand, I felt like a cultural anthropologist unearthing long-forgotten treasures. I captured the booty on film and repeated the oft-asked question uttered by many before me. "Who will lead the people?" I didn't know who would bring them into the future, but I thought that maybe, just maybe, I could show them part of their past.

floating 1

Lights dim, Marvin Gaye's syrupy thick, sad voice reached through me as I lay on the futon in the bedroom of my apartment studying the canvas holding the black-and-white image of the trees. Sipping gin, I thought of colors. Began with the sky blue of my mother's hydrangeas. That was the bass line since my mother was my earth, the source of my spring, my starting point, the foundation upon which my every effort was built. The irony of co-opting the Five Percenter's phrase and calling a white woman my earth struck me as funny, and I laughed, thinking about how even as bad as we are to the earth, it never leaves us the way my mother did.

In my mind, sky blue streaked with white reminded me of the hope I had felt before the first time I fell down. The time I had stepped big under the sun, feeling like I belonged, before I came crashing to the earth like Adam and Eve when they first learned of their nakedness.

"I hear you, Marvin," I say to my soulmate.

Yellow. Like the sun. Like daffodils. Like baby chicks. Like the innocent laughter of children whose temperaments haven't yet been colored by the world. Like crème brûlée. Like my skin, the pale skin that traps my tortured soul inside. Like the skin I want to destroy.

Like my skin before I press my fingers into it. Like my skin before it erupts into red marks, the shadows that follow the pressure left by my hands, which are inherently gentle but made rough from use. Like me.

"I love you, Marvin."

Red. Vibrant. Powerful. Rich. Fatiguing. It screams, "See me. Notice me. I am important." Like blood. Like the tracks of blood that I've made with a sewing needle on the inner, upper part of my arm. Away, where no one can see it. Near my breast. Where no one can see it readily. Unless in the fit of passion I fling my arms back beyond my head in sweet surrender. And my visitors never inspire that kind of passion. They are just noise and space-fillers. My arm, near my breast. When have I felt that kind of surrender? Near my breast. Never. My breast.

"Marvin, come closer. Come into my heart."

Brown. Open. Trusting. Unpretentious. Reacting when stimulated or aroused or provoked. Then it will rise, pointing, accusing, waiting to be covered. Otherwise cool. Brown can be solitary like its cousin black, assuming the role of the last man standing, but it will soon succumb because it doesn't have the strength to stand alone. Its weakness gets overshadowed by its cousin.

"Touch me there, Marvin."

Black. The sum of all colors whose murkiness is opaque, but for me, it's definite unlike this weak cream, tan, yellow skin that holds me hostage, never letting me go too far this way or that. Not white. Not black. Stuck in hapless limbo. It cannot be seen through. It's a mystery. It can't be compared, comprehended, contrasted, constructed, deconstructed, demystified, denounced, dethroned, overthrown, outshone, outgrown, outnumbered, outgunned, undone. It's the sum of all colors. It's the sum of all fears. It's night. It's mourning. Mourning. Mourning.

70

"Marvin, take me."

Sky blue hope turned to navy despair, and the blue grief swirled with black creating a sorrowful violet too intense to be contained.

"Take me with you, Marvin, so I don't feel this pain anymore."

once more

It was Friday, and I wanted to see him once more before the week-end claimed him. Camera in hand, I headed toward my usual spot after my 11:30 African American Lit Class ended. Gladfelter Hall on 12th Street was the only place on campus where I didn't feel quite so different. It housed the African American Studies Department, and from the moment I stepped off the elevator onto the eighth floor, I felt at home. Except my own home was not this warm. Leaving Gladfelter felt like leaving a cocoon, but it was okay. I could feel a similiar heat radiate from him, and I knew that I would feel it even more once I was actually able to get close to him.

As I walked up Montgomery toward 12th, something felt different. I felt his presence, but I knew I shouldn't have felt it so soon. I checked my watch. Twelve forty-five. He was early.

I slowed my pace and scanned the street looking for him. I spotted him on the other side of the street, approaching 12th. He waved at me as he passed. I waved back, hoping that his feet would guide him to me. Instead, once he reached 12th, he turned left and headed south.

And I was left with my camera in hand, wondering why.

with racing heart 2

With racing heart,
I stepped inside.
Nice day for a hot
air balloon ride.
Wanted to see
the city's sights,
explore them from
the highest heights.
Others, they quaked,
fearfully shook,
covered their eyes,
and couldn't look.
Not me, the rush
shot through my veins.
Got bold, wanted
to take the reins.
Instead I stood
close to the edge,
tempting my fate,
a privilege.

Lifting my hands
up to the sky,
I closed my eyes,
dreamed that I'd fly
away from hurt
away from pain.
Why live much more,
nothing to gain?
Touched down on earth
Looked 'round to see
if he was there
to rescue me.

work

"I'll pay for tuition and nothing else," my father had said when I told him the summer before my sophomore year that I wanted to live in an apartment. Wounded pride wouldn't allow me to contact my mother, so I knew that I needed a job then to pay rent and utilities and to buy food. Occasionally, I did freelance photos for a local black paper, but ironically, the steady job that paid regularly thrust me right into the kind of photography I hate. The staged, preposed high school yearbook style. My job was doing posed family portraits at a low-end department store in The Gallery, urban Philadelphia's excuse for a mall.

Three days a week, I watch the people file in like an unruly band of ragtag troops. The mother is almost always the lone general, ordering and yanking her cadets in line and hissing commands through lips clenched thin with anger. I regard the women, who are either worried thin with anxiety or swollen with desolation. Just as I feel myself grow weary with their hopelessness, a father accompanies his wife, girlfriend, or baby's mama to the photo shoot, and I go about my business, arranging children with stamped-on smiles who have been warned to behave and to act their age not their color.

I marvel at the way the mothers can sweep the fatigue from their cheeks, their lips, and their shoulders, but it never disappears from their eyes. They smile prettily, innocently for the few moments it takes for me to capture the image, but when I'm done, so are they. Their masks are off, and they are again tired generals, ordering children about through lips clenched thin with anger.

I marvel at the way the fathers, with children and baby's mama in tow, can look at me with questions in their eyes, only turning away when I show lack of interest. For them, these fathers who surely are tired, too, the questions stem from the feeling of being trapped. These questions ask for asylum, plead for the temporary shelter of being wrapped in my arms and legs. They think that they'll find solace in the arms of a cream-colored woman who many regard as a dream. They don't know, they can't know, that I'm as unhappy as they are, even more so. As much as I despise the cookie-cutter term, sometimes I feel like the epitome of the tragic mulatto destined to wander the world in search of happiness. I have nothing to give, and as some of the men look at me, I try to force the vacancy of my soul into my eyes to tell them that. Instead, they see hazel eyes set in skin like crème brulee decorated with a thin nose and pouty, suckable lips adorning a face framed by amber locks that curl dangerously, flowing beyond my shoulders. Their questioning eyes follow the path of my hair down my back, and although my tresses stop well above my behind, their eyes continue to roam down to my behind which is as tight as their girlfriends' used to be before she gave him the gift of children. Then, they are reminded that their children and baby's mamas are there with them. And they look at these ghosts of women, busying themselves by pulling rumpled bills from their purses. And they silently acknowledge the sacrifices of these worn women before kissing them on their tired, tired eyes. And they collect their offspring and leave the store. And the men will never know that the women saw them admiring my perceived beauty. And they'll never know of the ugliness trapped inside of me.

words

He knew that it was time to exchange words with me, but I could tell as he approached that he didn't know which words to offer. Suave? Sincere? Charming? Candid? Should he approach using his intellect? Approach me with caution? As a friend? A future lover? He tossed the thoughts about, registering every one of them on his face.

"Hi," he said, sitting next to me on the bench near the library.

"Hey," I returned, wiping my hands on a napkin to remove any traces of pizza sauce from them. I tossed the napkin toward the trash can, missing it. A bold squirrel came to my rescue, curiously pushing the napkin around, searching for crumbs.

"Not much of an athlete, huh?" he laughed.

"Nope. You know what they say. White girls can't jump."

He laughed again, studying me before saying, "The sister in you should at least be able to hit the rim."

"The brother in you sure knows how to talk trash."

"Only when I know the person I'm talking to is tough enough to handle it."

The early spring wind teased us, licking us lightly as we took juvenile introductory jabs at each other.

"So you like taking pictures of me, huh?" he asked. He didn't sound cocky or scared. Just curious. His earnestness compelled me to answer him honestly.

"You're a good subject to study. Intense, but not too overpowering. Focused. Graceful. If I could describe a person as moving magically, you're it."

He smiled at me, eyes squinting slightly as if I were now his subject to study. "I'm Lionel Jackson," he said, offering his hand.

"Shanna Washington," I returned, taking his hand firmly.

"Ooh, hearty handshake. None of that soft, flirty stuff with you."

"I don't flirt. It's a waste of time. If I have something to say, I say it."

"Direct. That's a plus."

"I didn't know you were doing a checklist," I commented wryly.

"Aren't we always?"

"Only if you have a goal or a game in mind."

"You mean to tell me that you never make mental notes?"

"Mental notes, yes. Checklists, no. I don't play games, so I don't approach people like a 'things-to-do' list."

He sat quietly before admitting, "I do."

"To each his own," I said, holding up the peace sign as a truce.

We talked for ten minutes more before I gathered my things to head down to The Gallery Mall. As I stood and lifted my bag to my shoulder, he stood, too.

"Can I have your number before you go?"

"Nope, I'll give it to you the next time I see you," I said, turning to leave.

"Is it like that?" he asked, trying to gauge my attitude and level of interest.

"Naw, it's not like that. I just want to talk to you face-to-face before I hit you off with my number."

As I walked away, I turned casually back just in time to see the smile creeping across his chiseled face.

running

"So where do you go when you run?" I asked, looking into Lionel's eyes.

"It depends on my mood," he said, staring boldly back.

"Explain."

He looked down for a second, as if gathering strength. "I run north on 12th Street when I'm trying to remember . . ."

"Remember what?" I asked interrupting.

"When I'm trying to remember my roots and where I've been."

"And you run south on 12th when . . . ?"

"I run south when I'm trying to forget."

"What are you trying to forget, Lionel?" I asked, looking directly into his eyes, waiting.

"The same thing everyone else is trying to forget. The past."

I accepted his response without pushing further, and we spent the rest of the afternoon lounging on Kelly Drive where I took pictures of boats passing along the Schuylkill River. As his hand came to rest on my thigh, I felt his heat combine with my own, and the result for me was almost explosive.

floating 2

I have stars on my ceiling, but I can see them only when the lights are off and it's dark. And as I lay on my back, staring up at the stars and sipping some brandy, I wonder if the stars ever get lonely. There are so many of them, but they are spread apart. I wonder, do they have hearts that crave company like I do? Do they long for the heat that only another star can bring? Do they want to pry themselves loose from their fixed celestial spots and move slightly, ever so slightly, across the heavens to another star that resembles them? Feels them? And once joined, will the new and improved larger star shine brighter? Will it pulsate and throb, growing more luminous with each silent vibration? Will it glow and grow in intensity that feels like the walls are collapsing inward? Will it scream out in passion as it starts its descent, exhausted, falling from the sky? Will it smear orgasmic star juice across the heavens, leaving a trail for us to remember that there once stood a refulgent, brilliant star that was the brightest that the sky had to offer? Will we remember it when it's gone?

lionel's dad

"When I think about it, he was never really a father to me," Lionel began.

I searched for bitterness in his words, but it was absent. They were just words telling a story, unraveling a life.

"It was almost like he used my mother as a rest stop. Only he stayed long enough to plant me in her womb. He was from the neighborhood, and he worked odd jobs."

My puzzled look prompted him to explain.

"Sometimes, men who don't have steady jobs gather on a corner early in the morning, and guys who need day laborers come around in vans to pick up some workers. So that's what my dad did. He didn't have a real profession.

"My mother said that she'd always known about his drinking, but when he settled in with her, he at least gave her part of his pay. After he'd hit the liquor store, of course, and she was satisfied with that. She says that she'd never intended to get pregnant, but when she did, the thought of me gave her hope. She talked about me to the neighbors, predicting all of the great things I'd do with my life. She even did something that she'd seen on television but thought was silly. She read to me in the womb. She didn't have many books around the house, but she read from the only book that she had. The Bible. She wasn't even particularly religious, but she said that she had to read something.

"She says that my dad even slowed down his drinking a little in preparation for my arrival. But something happened. In the course of reading the Scriptures, she started imbibing some of the teachings. Then, she could never look at my father the same way. She started pressuring him to get married and to get a real job. She wanted him to straighten up and be a man of The Word. She told him that when his son, for she just knew that I was a boy, claimed his place in the world, he would be more respected if he could point to married parents as his source of strength. So, my father married her so that I could have a name and dignity. He tried to stand straight, but he wouldn't get what my mother called a decent job.

"When I was little, about two or three, she sat me down and started teaching me my letters. She expected my father to help her, and that was when she realized that he couldn't read. He was so humiliated that he plunged back into the bottle again, and this time, he never climbed out."

I sat quietly as Lionel's words sank in. Now I knew why he never drank. He was afraid that the addiction ran in his genes, and he didn't want to tempt fate. Like me, he had been abandoned by a parent, but unlike me, he hadn't been broken by that abandonment. He used it to fuel him. He had hope. But me, I had nothing. So I latched on and dived in like a kid doing a cannonball. And I hoped that he could save me and take me to higher ground.

i saw

Learning about him was easy because he had no pretenses. He spoke plainly, and as he spoke, I saw his heart.

I saw where he had been, and I knew that the poverty of his youth had made him as out of place as I had felt throughout my childhood. He had leapt over the land mines of ignorance that had surrounded him. Street corner prophets, he called them, had filled the air around the slums with tirades about the devilish white man and his constant oppression. Meanwhile these same prophets had looked away, averting their eyes from the hustlers indiscriminately distributing their merchandise to anyone who had the money to buy it. Those same hustlers had sold the killer dose of heroin to Lionel's father, who would have died of AIDS sooner or later anyway.

I saw where he was now, a college junior who had gotten where he was by keeping his nose clean. He was hardened, though, and the hardness in his eyes was ominous and sometimes threatening. Discipline had gotten him the track scholarship that was paying for his education, and discipline was what earned him a 3.6 g.p.a. He sometimes seemed to long for the comfort of a home that existed only in his mind. North Philly's badlands had never been his home, it was simply where he resided. Once you were able to get out of there, you never went back because it crushed dreams and dreamers. He was set to begin a summer internship with the mayor's office, and the potential of his bright future exhilarated him and inspired me.

I saw his vision for his future, and I was proud of him. Politics was his dream, for he knew that it was the only vehicle through which change would come. Politics was everything, and everything was politics. Educational programs ... politics. Funding for community programs ... politics. Funding for medical research ... politics. Stronger police presence ... politics. He knew that he had to be in the loop in order to hobnob with those in the know and make the connections he needed. He had no family friends to fall back on who could help him with his career aspirations. But I saw the hope in his eyes, so I promised to take him with me on some of my photography gigs for the local black papers. I wanted nothing more than to see him bloom, but I didn't know then, couldn't know, that as he bloomed, I would wilt.

the first night

Six o'clock found me back in my apartment where I had already showered and slathered my body in vitamin E oil. I slipped into some black leggings, a black sleeveless turtleneck, and black mules, and I wrapped a blue sarong around my hips and adorned myself with turquoise jewelry before heading out of my apartment and walking over to Lionel's place.

Peace, Lionel's fellow track team member and roommate, was shoveling the last bit of mac and cheese from the pot into his mouth when Lionel opened the door.

"Hi," he said. "This is a nice surprise."

"Hey," I returned, stepping into the room. "What's up, Peace?"

"You. Comin' in here lookin' all scrumptious and wrecking a brother's concentration," he said, licking his full lips and wiping his face with a honey-colored hand.

"Back off, Brick," Lionel warned, shortening the nickname of Peace's hometown of Newark, New Jersey, and kicking a pile of clothes under his roommate's bed.

"I guess that since you tidyin' up and shit, that's my cue to be out," Peace observed, gathering his books. "If wassername calls, tell her I'll swing through later," he said, closing the door behind him.

I leaned on the door that Peace had just closed and watched Lionel as he finished highlighting some lines in his textbook. Smiling, he looked up at me.

"You gonna stand way over there by the door?"

"Guess what I did today?" I asked ignoring his question.

"What?"

"Something spontaneous and crazy," I hinted, removing my sarong.

He looked intrigued and anxious as I rested my thumbs in my waistband.

"What?" he repeated.

Slowly I eased the pants down from my hips, just enough for him to get a glimpse of the sleek smoothness of my hairless kitty.

"Word!" he exclaimed as he walked toward me. He kneeled down before me and rested his hands on my thighs. "Let me see the whole thing," he whispered hungrily, waiting for me to remove my pants and give him the go-ahead.

"It's yours," I responded, kicking the ball into his court.

That was all the prompting he needed. He slid my pants down as I kicked off my mules, and without any hesitation, he lifted my right leg over his shoulder and slipped his tongue into the hairless creases of my womanhood. His tongue danced lazily over my clit, which was already hardening from anticipation of his play. He cupped my ass, balancing my weight in his hands.

The moisture collecting between both sets of lips caused me to suck my teeth as I slurped in my saliva. He slurped in my juice as his tongue continued to dart about. Escalating ecstasy impelled me to rock my pelvis rhythmically into his face, and I felt the sensational burn of an orgasm beginning in the pit of my being. I heard the whimper trickle from my throat, growing louder and louder until it erupted into unrestrained, throaty screams of passion. I clamped my raised leg around his head, and he held me until my shivering subsided, and I sank to the floor.

He wiped his mouth and looked at the clock before smiling at me. "Baby, I hate to eat and run, but I've got a study group that started fifteen minutes ago."

"Oh," I said, standing up to slide my pants back on. I kissed him, tasting my juice on his tongue, as I rewrapped my sarong on my hips.

He grabbed a washcloth from his closet and picked up his shower caddy. As he ushered me through the door and into the hallway, Peace, standing in the middle of a group of his teammates at the end of the hall, began to applaud loudly. The other guys joined him, cheering enthusiastically as Lionel kissed me on my forehead and slapped my ass as I exited the dorm from the side entrance.

lionel said

After the first time we made love, Lionel said:

"What I like about you, Shanna, is that you're so patient. You only speak when you have something to say, and you don't rush me with my thoughts. You give me time to sort through my thoughts before I speak. You don't press me or depress me with useless complaints or whining about things that can't be changed. You just accept what's to be accepted and reject bullshit that's not worthy of your time or energy. You stay calm, or at least you're calm on the surface. Of course I know that saying, 'Still waters run deep.' You'll talk to me in your own time, though, and I know that your thoughts will be airtight, crisp perfection like you. You have no hidden agendas. You're not out to get anything from anybody. You work hard, and someday, all that hard work will pay off. You know that, and I know that, and that makes all the difference in the world. Some women try to trap guys into saying and doing things that they don't have the heart or the desire to do. But not you, Shanna. It's like you're innocent and trusting, and that's refreshing. You keep it real, right down to the way you look. You don't put all of that shit in your hair, trying to be something you're not. Old-school cats might say that you are as fine as wine with your redbone, brickhouse self. Your skin is like butter, and you make a brother want to melt when you look at him with those pretty-ass eyes. To top it off, you've got a head full of good hair. You're the kind of woman who belongs on the arm of a politician, an attorney, a businessman, or a university president. You wouldn't be worrying him with petty bullshit, either. You'd just stand there by his side looking pretty in front of people. Then, at night, you'd let him curl himself up into your arms like I am now. And you'd let him lay his worries at your feet and put his heart in your hands. Like a real woman. That's what I like about you, Shanna."

i wanted to say . . .

"...I'm not patient. I just don't have the heart to act on things the way I probably should. I have a whole lot to say, but I'm too much of a coward, and I'm afraid that my words and actions have the power to drive people away. So, yeah, I do accept what's to be accepted because I learned long ago that my wants don't matter.

"...and you're wrong about the hidden agenda. The only item on my agenda is love, but I don't know if I'll ever get it, or if I'm even worthy.

"...and here we go again with the light skin, pretty eyes, good hair bullshit. Brother, be original. I hate to admit it, but you're as brainwashed as the rest, including my father. And when the time and opportunity come, you'll replace me with someone even lighter to shore up your status.

"...and, yeah, you're right. Still waters do run deep."

a memory

Sometimes when the words in my textbooks are a blurry haze, and music can't penetrate my soul, I sit in silence in the sanctuary of my apartment, and thoughts come to me. They swish in like waves, each one flowing deeper, leaving a vague imprint that I struggle to bring to life. So many ghosts of past and present mixed with a haze of smoke have clouded my mind that I grapple to remember what's real and what's not. But this memory keeps coming back, so I know that it must be a true memory.

We, my mother, my father, and I, are getting ready to go see a production of Langston Hughes' *Black Nativity*, an annual production staged by Freedom Theater. I sit in my usual spot under the dining room table where I'm playing with colored plastic strips my mother calls "gamp" but my father calls "gimp." I'm weaving the strips into a keychain and peeking intermittently at my father who is reading the back cover of a new blues album. I hear my mother humming as she descends the stairs, and I see her stockinged tan legs and black high heels as she stands in the foyer between the two rooms. I hear a beautiful crash of shells emanate from her clothing, and I peek up to see my mother in a rush of colors. The vibrant African fabric of her caftan makes her light skin seem pale, but she's beautiful anyway.

She lifts her bangled arms and becomes a marvelous butterfly. Fabric is wound around her head, and blond strands hang in curly tendrils from the edges of her head wrap. She looks so happy. I am about to crawl from under the table to hug her when I hear my father's gruff voice.

"Go take that off."

The beautiful beads stop their clanging, and her legs are still.

"It's festive, honey. I thought it would be a nice touch."

"I said, go take it off."

In my stillness, I can feel the smile fall from her lips. Stunned, she doesn't move. But he does.

He is on her in a flash, and her beautifully bangled arm, which had been lifted gracefully, is bent behind her back, her wrist twisted between her shoulder blades. I see her knees bent in submission, and her voice is a whimper. His feet are planted firmly behind her.

"Where's Shanna? Wh-where's Shanna?" she whispers, a plea in her voice.

Ignoring her question, he says in a voice like ice, "Don't you mock me, Main Line. I said take that shit off. Now go do it."

"O-okay," she stutters with tears in her throat.

Just as quickly as he pounced, he walks away, going outside to start the car. My mother scampers up the steps, and I scurry from under the table. When she comes back down, I am in the kitchen in front of the open freezer, trying to freeze my tears. She walks in wearing black slacks, a black sweater, and pearls. Her hair is held back by a headband, and she looks normal, save for the redness in her eyes.

floating 3

With the spring air wafting into my bedroom, I lay quietly drinking bourbon while Gil Scott-Heron spoke to me from a different place and time. Behind my closed lids I saw his golden skin, not much darker than mine, and I felt the confusion that coursed through his veins. America, place of prosperity and poverty. Oasis of opportunity and oppression. Land of liberty and lynchings. How could such a place exist? How could such a dichotomy divide one very real truth from the other very real truth? If opportunity is simply grasping the reigns at the time they're thrown your way rather than waiting until you're ready to assume them, why can't people stand at the ready, anticipating the moment they'll hit the ground, ready to run? Is there really a divide then? Is there really a black side and a white side? Is there really such a keen split between right and wrong? Or is it just a matter of where one is standing when the question is asked? And if we sometimes venture to the wrong side, is there no redemption for us?

introductions 1

I flashed my press credentials to the hostess at the reception table, and Lionel, carrying my camera bag, eased into the door behind me. Looking around the foyer of Belmont Mansion, he was a sponge, absorbing the sights, sounds, and smells of power.

"Let's roll," I asserted, leading him into the reception room where the new secretary of labor and industry was being feted by his former colleagues from the Equal Employment Opportunity Commission.

Hope gleamed in Lionel's eyes as he listened to me rattle off names and gesture at the "must meets" gathered in the room.

"... attorney who handles that foundation with art on loan to the museum ... cop turned doctor who has his hand in everything of importance in the city ... federal judge and his wife the stockbroker ... president of Lincoln University ... partner at Dutton, Collins and Kind who just handled that transportation authority case ..."

He salivated at opportunity upon opportunity and moved in confidently, pressing the flesh of the members of the other face of Philadelphia power. As he made his way around, I circled in the other direction, reintroducing myself, arranging people for quickie flicks, and jotting names and notes into my pocket notepad. We met briefly between each round, nibbled on hors d'oeuvres and exchanged names to know. If I hadn't been working, I would have almost considered the evening fun.

After two hours we climbed back into my Wrangler and headed back to Temple. As I navigated my way down the open expanse of I-76, Lionel sifted through the business cards he had collected, holding them as if they were gold.

shaping me

With my hand locked in his, we meandered through Willow Grove Mall, a three-story, suburbanite's shopping paradise. Shopping was not high on my list of priorities, but for Lionel, image was everything. Even though he didn't have much money, he enjoyed dreaming as he window-shopped. I thought window-shopping was a colossal waste of time, but, as usual, I said nothing.

He eyed the Jil Sander racks in Bloomingdale's, taking a pretty piece from one and holding it up before me.

"What do you think of this?"

"It's nice," I responded, looking at the ensemble.

"This would look good on you," he continued, nudging me toward the mirror. "Classy."

"Mm-hmm," I pretended to agree. The outfit, though exquisite and elegant, looked too Main Line for my artistic taste.

"This is what I'd like to see you wear," he commented. "And when you straighten your hair, you'll look like a knockout."

"What's wrong with my hair?" I asked, trying to keep the edge out of my voice.

"Nothing. It's just a little wild, but it's nothing that a blow-dryer or a hot comb can't tame," he smiled. "Then, you'd be fit to be on the arm of anyone, especially a young, handsome politician."

He took the clothes from me and replaced them on the rack, leaving me looking at my unfit image in the mirror.

the call

The call came when I was developing my pictures from the reception that Lionel and I attended. When I emerged from the darkroom, I checked my messages. On my machine, the words crawled out of his mouth like icebergs drifting on the sea, slurred by Old Grand-Dad.

"You need to come home."

That was it. Five words that spoke volumes. Five words that said he needed me.

With racing heart, I jumped into my jeep and sped north on Broad Street, through chaos and back to comfort because my father needed me. He needed me.

The door was open when I got there, like a mouth agape, waiting to be filled. I entered softly, expecting to find him in a heap on the living room floor. Instead, he sat in his chair, head thrown back and mouth twisted in what looked like a smile, though tears charged out the sides of his eyes, racing toward his ears.

I reached toward him, wrapping my arms around his head.

I felt the shudder of his body before he erupted like a wailing volcano. Dashing his glass against the wall, he pounded the arms of his chair wildly before allowing his arms to settle around my back. I nestled against him until I felt the shaking subside. Then I dried his tears with my hair, a variation of what the whore had done for Jesus, the most tender and humble act of selflessness that a woman can show. I crumbled into a ball at his feet and waited for him to speak.

"Your grandmother died tonight. She was shot during an argument in the bar across the street from her house. She died in the street before I got there. Imagine that. Sixty-five years old, and getting shot down like a dog. That's not supposed to happen. No old person is supposed to die a death like that. Once you reach a certain age, when the time comes, you're supposed to pass with dignity, not like some common thug. She still shames me. Even in death, she shames me."

going home

He took the train to Virginia the next day, returning to the place his mother had fled all those years ago. I had told him that I'd drive down after my final exam, which would put me in Hampton two days before the funeral. He nodded and shrugged, looking much smaller than I had ever seen him look. Then he stepped gingerly onto the train in 30th Street Station, and I had stood on the platform, frantically waving good-bye to him the way lovers do after whispering, "Until we meet again." He waved simply before turning and looking ahead, signaling our return to formality.

I had told Lionel that he could stay in my apartment while I was gone, and knowing that the dorms were belching out students who'd return to their homes for the summer and knowing that his mother's rented house in the badlands would suffocate him, he agreed.

As I thought of Lionel's options, my own mother passed through my mind, and I toyed with the idea of calling her. I didn't know what I'd say, and my heart quaked at the notion of reaching out to the woman who'd abandoned me, so instead, I checked the jeep's registration to get my mother's address and dropped a note in the mail to her, informing her of my grandmother's demise. I knew not to expect any empty expression of condolence from her. In fact, I didn't even know what to feel myself because my father's mother was simply a genetic connection. No emotions tied her to me because my father had severed those strings long before I was born.

Exams behind me, I departed Philadelphia, traveling down 95 South to 495 to 13 South where I stopped every so often to buy fruit from rickety stands and soft-shell crab sandwiches and steamed shrimp from anonymous fish houses dotting the landscape. The wind whipped across my face and through my hair, enveloping me in the comforting smell of salty seawater. Dusk found me emerging from the Chesapeake Bay Bridge Tunnel, and on my cell phone I called my father's uncle to clarify my directions. He guided me to Hampton, and when I set foot on solid ground, I felt the click of familiarity through blood memory.

This place had never been a part of my consciousness, but it was my family's home, and it was in my blood. I was yearning for my roots, and I hoped that being with my family would satiate some of my longing.

Uncle Joe, my grandmother's twin, strode over to me, saying, "Hey, girl," as he took me in his arms. He smelled of saltwater and hair pomade, and as he squeezed me, images of sand, rope, and cornfields flashed through my mind. He felt like home, and in my longing to stay in his arms, I held on too long. He mistook my clinging for grief, and patting me on the back, he spoke through lips like my father's. "You'll be alright, girl. You'll be just fine."

before the funeral

"That was one hard woman," my father commented to the night air, for he had returned to the place where he didn't talk to me. He talked to other people, but he talked at me. Talking to requires the speaker to pause for input. It implies that the listener has something of import to add. Talking at is more of a monologue of sorts. A soliloquy. I listen closely, though, because sometimes things are revealed in the speech that would never be said in an equal exchange of conversation.

"She was a hell-raiser. As the old folks would say, 'She wouldn't take no tea for the fever.' Would cut a man in a heartbeat, and women were smart enough not to cross her." He smiled a soft smile when he said that, like he was holding a good memory of her. Just as softly, his smile faded away.

"But sometimes, sometimes, she would turn out for no reason at all, and it was embarrassing. Her mouth was filthy. She'd cuss you six ways from Sunday. Shameless. She'd make you want to curl up in a ball, but even that wasn't safe, being in a ball in her womb. She'd shake you loose in a minute, like she never owned you, but all you wanted was for her to hold your hand, stroke your hair, or rub your back. But she'd never give you that. Even though that was all you needed. That would be too personal, too motherly, too much like she loved you and you mattered."

He spat at the sidewalk which was spotted with tobacco stains.

"She ain't in heaven, that's for sure. You can't run around here cutting and cussing people and expect to see the pearly gates. Oh no. God's got something for that. It's called hell, and she's probably down there giving the devil a run for his money. Shit, she probably owns the place by now." He chuckled before taking a drag on his cigar.

Anger flashed across his face like lightning as he forced the smoke from his lungs.

"All those times. All those reports from people laughing at her and at me. Telling me that they saw her here or there, turning the place out. I couldn't go anywhere without somebody telling me that they saw my mother behaving as wild as a park ape. No damn dignity in her whole body."

He took another drag from his cigar.

"Running my father away. Running me away. And one day she had the nerve to ask why."

browning

I lay on a blanket in the yard, browning myself under the Southern sun. Relatives I never knew I had swarmed about the house, embracing my father like the prodigal son and me through association. A little cousin plopped herself on the blanket near my head and pulled at my hair, stretching out one of the curls and admiring the length of the amber lock before releasing it and saying "Boing" as it sprang back to its curled state. Her childlike giggle inspired a chuckle from me, and I reached up, hugging her maternally before shooing her away.

Then I thought of my own mother, wondering how, though space and circumstance separated us, I would respond if I learned that she had passed away. My heart said no, and it began to lead my mind through a web of memories as I drifted off to sleep.

I was nudged awake by the same little cousin who commanded, "Flip over. You're pretty done on this side."

Rolling over, I laughed again before returning to my daydream.

after the funeral

A few days after the funeral, Uncle Joe sat on the front porch, or garret as he called it, with me and my father. As I rocked lazily in a chair, I searched my palate for vestiges of sweet potato pie that I had eaten for an afternoon snack.

"Has the family always lived in Hampton?" I asked, wondering if we had any ties to the university.

"Of course not, child," he sputtered, looking at me like the question was the most asinine thing he had ever heard. "Didn't your grandmother tell you how we ended up in Hampton?"

I looked to my father for help, but his face was a waiting canvas. I didn't know how to tell this man in dress slacks, suspenders, and a "Number 1 Grandpa" shirt, who had shared his home with us for almost a week, that the first time I laid eyes on his sister, my grandmother, was as she lay in her coffin. The hard words would surely break his heart. I simply gulped and replied, "No, sir."

"We came here when we were almost seven years old. It was right after our father died, and our mother's sister took us all in."

Ignorance forced me into silence as I waited for the gaps to be filled.

"Our momma and daddy hadn't officially married when she got

pregnant with us. Of course, that was a mark of shame then. We didn't do things like they do it now, all wrong and bold about it. Well, my daddy married her as soon as he knew she was with child, and he set them up in a house on the edge of Courtland on the Wadsworth farm over in Southampton County. Well, he was share-cropping, so it wasn't like he owned the house or anything, but he tried to make a way for them anyway.

"After we were born and we started growing, Daddy saw that his wages were just enough to keep the family one mouthful shy of starving, and he felt helpless. Yeah, we nibbled on the crops he grew, but when you're dependent on those crops for your livelihood, you try to sell as much as you can. Well, he got it in his mind to come north because it was supposed to be this promised land where col-ored folks could walk around with pride and a man could feel like a man. So he went to tell Mr. Wadsworth about his plans.

"Mr. Wadsworth was a man who was just holding on. He was barely holding on to his land since in WWI the army took so many colored in their ranks, and believe it or not, he was running low on help. Then, one of his sons got back from the war, and he was a walking vegetable. After a few years of carrying on, he blew his brains out right in front of his daddy. The other son fled the South, hoping to increase the family's wealth in real estate. Then with the Depression hitting, Mr. Wadsworth got knocked down again. That was a lot for a man to bear, but then again it doesn't take much for white people to break. Well, anyway, he just saw everything around him crumbling, so when our father came to him to tell him about his plans for leaving, story goes he just looked at him and said real calm, 'Naw, you ain't.' That night, he came to our house and called my father outside. He shot my father dead right in front of this house. Then he got back on his horse and went back to his own house where he told his wife that the world was changing too fast for him.

"Momma was a widow now, and she tried to find a way to keep her family afloat. She went to Mrs. Wadsworth and tried to appeal to her, woman to woman, for some help or something. Mrs. Wadsworth told her that she had her husband to thank for her predicament and if she didn't get off of her property by sunrise, she'd make us orphans. So we left Courtland and headed to Hampton where our Aunt Sissy lived."

Uncle Joe shook his head with disbelief at the woman's coldness, and I waited for him to continue.

"Momma didn't give herself enough time to lick her wounds. Before we knew it she was out trying to find work. She found work, shucking crabs at a canning factory, and one night as she was walking home, some men offered her a ride. They took her to a farm by Buckroe Beach, and they had their way with her all night. In the morning, somebody found her in the cornstalks, and they brought her home. Aunt Sissy nursed her back to health, and we all thought she was getting better, but she commenced to talking about having white men's poison in her, saying that she had to get it out. Nobody knew what she was talking about, and we all thought she was talking out of her head. Then one day, we came home from school . . ."

He paused, swiping at his eyes, and I knew that the words he had to tell were like a stone sitting at the bottom of his stomach. Telling the story would be like purging, and after the words were out of his stomach, he would be free. But I didn't know how to coax the story out of him, and neither did my father, who sat, head in hands, looking at the ground. Looking at them, it hit me how much the two men resembled. Now I knew where the looks had come from, and it felt like puzzle pieces were coming together. The words in Uncle

Joe's stomach would complete the picture. My hungry eyes implored him to speak, and obediently, he coughed up the rest of the narrative.

"My sister, your grandmother, found our momma hanging from a rope at the back of the house. She was naked, and for the first time we saw the bulge of her pregnant stomach. She had tried to cut away the poison that was growing inside of her, leaving slashes that looked like plaid all over her stomach. My sister always was more quiet than I was, but this scared her silent. She didn't say a word for a long time, and when she finally did speak again, she spoke in whispers. She left from down here when she was sixteen, and she headed to Philadelphia. She stood on the train platform in Newport News and whispered, 'Brother, I need to get my voice back.' Then, she left.

"She wrote me once a week for years, telling me about life in Philadelphia and her job working as a secretary for some big-time lawyer named Moore. She told me about a WWII vet named Sarge who was courting her, but she said she'd never marry him because she didn't want to end up dead like our momma. And she didn't want him to die trying to take care of her. Then, she stopped writing, and I got scared, so I came up to Philadelphia to check on her. I found that she had gotten her voice back, and I found that she had gotten herself poisoned."

He stopped talking and smiled at my father. Then he said, "But I guess you don't look so dangerous."

driving back

My father and I rode in silence most of the way home. I had put the doors back on my jeep in anticipation of his joining me, and he rode in relative comfort, moving only to replace the jazz tapes that played, dancing out onto the wind as we cruised north on Route 13. We ordered soft-shell crabs and hushpuppies at the same anonymous roadside shack, and I stopped to let him stretch his legs at a mall in Salisbury, Maryland.

I had been expecting things to be different and hoping for a change in our relationship, but the fortress around his heart remained intact. I still didn't know his thoughts, but I knew his blood. I knew where it had flowed, and I could trace it back eighty-five years now instead of his forty-five. Eighty-five was still small in the grand scheme of things, but it was a start.

My father's silence mirrored his mother's after her eyes had been thrust open. He, too, had been baptized by fire, learning of his grandfather's murder and his grandmother's self-inflicted lynching. I wondered if the weight of it was too much to bear, and I reached across the divide of the jeep, seeking to close the gap of generations, gender, and race. The tips of my fingers grazed the back of his hand lightly first. Then my hand settled on his, nesting awkwardly, the bigger under the smaller. I felt the slight twitch of his hand like the rumble of a mighty elephant before it moves its massive body. I was scared that he would move my hand away, rejecting me all over again. I bit my lip, waiting for the ax to fall. Instead, in one fluid movement he moved his hand from the bottom to the top where it fit comfortably and made me warm from the inside out.

watching me

I sat cross-legged on the floor of the living room of my apartment, sorting through pictures and undoing my bra from underneath my T-shirt.

"How was the trip?" Lionel asked, lounging on a pillow near the balcony.

I reflected on my father holding my hand from Delaware to Philadelphia, and I said, "Despite the fact I went to a funeral, it was almost fine."

"Almost?"

"Yeah," I said, pausing to inhale. "I learned a lot of family history, and most of it was tragic, but at least I got to meet my people and I got to know my roots."

"Looks like you're trying to get back to your roots," he laughed, brushing his hand over my browned skin.

Annoyed, I sulked quietly, gulping from the glass of cheap wine that sat on the floor.

"Uh-oh. I guess I said something bad."

"You said something stupid."

"What's stupid about it, Shanna? I've always liked your skin color. It was pretty, like French vanilla ice cream. I just don't know why you'd want to get dark."

"This conversation is pointless and shallow, and I'm not going to continue it," I said, growing more aggravated. I closed my eyes, trying to forget that he was still in my space even though he should have been back in his home by now. Behind my closed lids, he was quiet, and my mind drifted back to Chesapeake Bay. The sun had shone differently as I lay on Virginia Beach, making me want to lap up its rays. Remembering the swish of the water licking at my toes, I wished that I was back there.

"Why do you drink?" he asked, breaking into my trance and wrecking my flow.

"Because it feels good," I responded, erasing the mounting edge from my voice.

"What do you think about when you're high?"

I looked at him, thinking, "You're determined not to let me have any peace." Removing the T-shirt and my sweats, I stood before him naked, allowing him to view my golden skin. I emptied the contents of the glass and sat on the floor.

"I think about this," I said, straddling him and preparing to sex him into submissive silence.

After I got him off, I poured another glass and walked into my bedroom, leaving him asleep on the floor.

what he wanted

As I got to know him better, I realized that what Lionel wanted was a highbrow woman. He wanted someone who, seemingly without effort, would appear manicured, pedicured, waxed, and curled by his side. He wanted a woman whose skin was flawless and whose hair would lay tamely on her shoulders before taking the plunge and cascading down her back.

I was a natural woman. The most I could do on my limited budget and sparse time was shave my legs and pluck my eyebrows. My hair was an amber halo, wild by design and free by choice.

What Lionel wanted was a woman who chatted intelligently and laughed daintily, interjecting witty anecdotes where appropriate. Someone charming. Someone fetching. Someone who would bolster but not overshadow him.

I was a quiet woman whose mind was twisted with sadness and loneliness. I rarely laughed, and when I did, it was loud and coarse like plates shattering. Like my father. I wasn't charming, but my beauty was enough for some.

What Lionel wanted was a woman whose clothes looked tailored and sculpted. Talbots and Ann Taylor were the stores he liked for me. Classic and clean was the look he preferred. A look that said he had arrived.

I was an artist, my look determined more by mood than style. Sometimes I'd wrap fabric around my waist and call it a skirt. A scarf became a shirt on a whim. I wasn't interested in 7th Avenue fashion or even Center City chic. Clothes, for me, were covering, a means of artistic expression.

What Lionel wanted was a woman who could whip together the gourmet meals that he had seen on one of the three hundred cable channels his mother watched in their rented shack. He desired someone whose domestic skills were dynamite, whose cleaning could pass the white glove test any day of the week.

I was proficient at keeping things suitable, which had been much easier before cleaning for two, since he didn't appear to want to leave after I returned from Virginia. Destinking the pee-streaked toilet and cleaning the soap-splattered sink and basin decorated with hair clippings and very-visible-he-must-be-fucking-blind toothpaste globs could be a full-time job. And food was nourishment to me, not art.

What Lionel wanted was someone who could give him the stability of home that he had craved all his life. I tried. Lord knows I tried because I wanted to lift him up. To see this black man whole. But what I could do was not enough. And sometimes he got angry. And in his anger, his words packed a mighty blow, and they sent me stumbling, left me reeling, made my head spin and my heart hurt with the familiarity I had known in childhood.

"You are such a fucking slob!"

"What the hell do you call that?"

"Look at what you're doing."

"Can't you do anything right?"

And oddly, there was comfort in that familiarity, so I stayed. After all, where else could I go? I was in my home.

watching him 1

I remembered that he said he runs north when he wants to remember and south when he wants to forget. I wanted to see what he sees when he runs, see what it is that haunts and inspires him. So one evening when he got home from work and had changed his clothes, I followed him in my jeep as he traveled north on 12th Street. For blocks I lagged behind or moved forward, perched stealthily on side streets or in alleys. I knew that going north would take him to his neighborhood, or maybe I should say his old neighborhood, since he seems to have moved in with me. No questions asked, no pacts made, just money on the kitchen counter when the electric bill comes and again when I mention needing groceries. Funny, that when the actual shopping had to be done, dinner made, laundry washed, and cleaning done, I did it alone.

Anyway, I took in the neighborhood as I drove through. The stamp of poverty and despair had been impressed upon the entire community, with its decaying buildings. Clicking my camera, I knew that if I submitted these photos with captions reading "Kabul," no one would question my facts because of the crumbling structures. They might wonder about the skinny black woman crouched, relieving herself between two soulless cars, and I'd explain that she was an indigenous woman performing a ritualistic expulsion regimen. The editors wouldn't know the difference.

Logically, I knew that Lionel would run from this blight, but my trip to Virginia taught me that swallowing poison over and over will just make your belly swell. The truth will come out eventually in the wash, so why pretend that it doesn't exist? Lionel's denying his roots was no more productive than my father's denying his: It wouldn't make a difference because the past would always haunt. So why not just make friends with the ghosts instead of denying their existence?

When I was ready to make myself known to Lionel, I pulled into the block that he was approaching and waited on the sidewalk, camera ready. He smiled when he recognized me, a repeat of the first time that he noticed me.

Click.

Concentration.

Click.

Anguish.

Click.

Drive.

Click.

Serenity.

Click.

Happiness.

Click.

A smile.

Click.

A wave.

Click.

A kiss blown my way.

Click.

Passing me by.

Click.

Nice ass.

Click.

Done.

watching him 2

He knew that since I had followed him north, I'd want to follow him south as well, so the next day he led me on the path to his southern mecca. And I saw why he was rushing to get there.

His steps led from bad to worse momentarily, and I felt like we were racing into the center of Dante's hellish circles. But after Vine Street the sun opened up, and we crossed through Chinatown, heading for Market. With him leading me through the stop-and-go traffic, we made a right onto Market Street and circled city hall, heading west toward 17th Street. My eyes glowed as I took in the sights of the city's skyscrapers and towers of trade and commerce. Of course, I had seen them all before, but never through Lionel's eyes.

At 17th we made a left, and I trailed him as he led me past the Westin Hotel, which is attached to the marble-floored Liberty Place Mall. He sprinted past the upscale eateries on restaurant row and the chic boutiques of the shopping district, and as we approached Walnut he signaled for me to make a right. We circled Rittenhouse Square, a pseudo Central Park situated in the center of brownstones, spas, five-star hotels, and high-rise condominiums with heated sidewalks. I parked the jeep as he circled the park again, and as I snapped his picture, his back looked straighter, his gait more assured, and his shoulders were at ease. The sun glistened off of his bronze skin, and he looked like a god. Then it clicked.

He wanted to be counted among the numbers of the elite that bartered and bargained in the City of Brotherly Love. He wanted to be counted, heard, and seen. He wanted to make his presence felt.

Viewing the world through his eyes, I was reminded again of his ambition, and it was admirable. His desire for success was so intense that even I could feel it. He was on his way, taking baby steps toward his dream. And despite his arrogance and my mounting annoyance with him, that day I wanted to see him get there. I wanted to be supportive and nurturing. A premonition warned me that if I stayed attached to him, his climb would be my descent, but that night when I met him in the shower with the showerhead on full blast, I wanted to wash away the stains of his past.

He devoured me with his eyes as I lathered my shower mitts with peppermint shower gel. I began with his hair, working the lather through his soft curls before gently nudging him under the streams of water. Stretching up, I licked his face, tasting the traces of salt as it mingled with minty suds and water. Then I moved my hands to his neck where I used the backs of my knuckles to knead the vertebrae at the base of his skull. Relathering, I massaged his broad bronze shoulders, and I felt the release of tension as my hands moved across his muscled back. My hands drifted to his front where I pretended to play a song on the chiseled washboard of his stomach. My hands danced down his abdomen toward his privates where I found his fat penis protruding like a massive cobra from the thick forest of curly hair. I circled it, playing hide and seek with it between my sudsy hands. Leaning down, I lathered his balls, manipulating them like silver Chinese stress balls between my fingers before I moved to the tops of his thighs, cleaning them with long, sweeping strokes. After lathering again, I rubbed his knees, his sensitive zone, in circular swipes, waiting for him to stop laughing. I cleaned his shins gently before moving on to his feet, which I exfoliated thoroughly, taking every toe between my fingers, and washing them. Standing, I turned him around, gently scrubbing the top of his high, mighty behind. I lathered his cheeks, lightly running my finger down the crevice that separated them. With his legs parted, I traversed the area between his cheeks, sliding my finger through his thighs and tickling his balls. As he chuckled, I finished cleaning him, cupped his cakes, and kissed his back before dismissing him from the bathroom and admonishing him to be ready when I got to the bedroom.

After quickly washing my body, I emerged from the shower, appearing in the bedroom doorway, smelling of mint and still dripping with warm water. I slid onto the bed next to him.

"You're wet," he murmured.

"I sure am," I cooed.

He kissed me hungrily, pulling my body to him so tightly that I felt myself melting into him. Ropes of hair twirled about as he rolled me onto my back. Effortlessly, I parted my legs, waiting for him to come to me. I heard the sound of the condom wrapper tearing as I gazed into the stars on the ceiling. He lowered his body onto mine, raining kisses down on me as I raised my knees and lifted my pelvis toward him, waiting to take him in. My hot juices bubbled with anticipation as he guided himself toward my womanhood. I felt him at the edge of my door, and as he eased inside of me, I thought I saw a star shoot across the heavens of my ceiling.

Lionel moved in me like a slow undulating wave, rising high, then sinking low. I met his solid thrusts with solid thrusts of my own. Each rhythmic collision sent a light sweep over my clitoris, and my groaning matched each plunge that he took into my wetness. Like waves we danced the erotic dance, arching our bodies and aching for pleasure. His thrusts grew in force, sinking deeper and deeper as he searched for the pearl within my walls. His breath quickened, and his movements became less sensual and more mechanical as he tried to bring himself to climax within me. I ceased being his lover and became his tool, and as I gripped him within my walls, his fervor grew. He pounded and pounded, poking imaginary holes into my womb.

He sucked his breath, whimpering, "Oh, God. Oh God. I'm about to . . . I'm about to . . ."

And his body went stiff, his electric rod reacting to the current within my wetness. He shook with passion, stilling his groans and momentarily stopping his breathing. He lay inside me until his stagnated breathing returned to normal. Then he withdrew, rolling over and sliding the sagging condom from his retracting penis. He tied a knot it in, lazily flinging it on the floor where it would stay until I discarded it in the morning. He wiped himself on my sheets, and before I could raise my voice in complaint, he was sleeping, snoring happily in the bliss of his afterglow.

introductions 2

"Shanna, the reception starts in twenty-five minutes," he called from the living room where he was finishing a bottle of apple juice.

I stifled the annoyance that was rising in me, threatening to yell, "Don't tell me what time the damn reception starts. I'm working the damn thing."

But so was he. It was his first mayoral reception, and his nerves had him checking his appearance and bellowing to me intermittently. The Pan-Hellenic Council was kicking off Greek Week with a Sunday service and a brunch reception at Bluezette's on Market Street. The mayor was a Kappa, and Lionel wanted to find favor in his eyes. He wanted to pledge Temple's chapter in the fall. The brotherhood that was shared among the collegiate and graduate members of the various fraternities and sororities was a compelling enough reason for Lionel to pledge. The underlying rationale, though, was that just about everyone in Philadelphia's black elite had pledged. It was like holding a Ph.D. at an Ivy League institution. Everyone had one, and it was assumed that anyone socializing in their company had one also. Lionel wanted desperately to belong, and he knew that this fraternal membership would open even more doors for him.

For months he had tried to get me interested in the idea of Greek life, but it was of no interest to me at all. As an only child, I wasn't used to being around a lot of people, and I didn't feel that a group of strangers making strange calls to each other and pledging undying love to two symbolic colors and long dead founders would complete me.

"You really should pledge AKA," he told me. "You've got the right look and everything."

"What look is that?" I demanded.

"Light skin, light eyes, long pretty hair . . ." he mused, amused with his shallow description of me.

"That's arbitrary and fickle," I said.

"Yeah, well that's what they used to go by. They claim that it doesn't matter anymore, but they'd sweat you so hard if you even casually mentioned joining their ranks, Shanna. You probably wouldn't even have to do the prerequisite mandatory community service."

"Just because I'm light-skinned, huh?"

"Because you've got that nonchalant, pretty girl look and attitude. For real. Think about it," he said as he stood in my living room jangling the keys to my apartment.

Now, I strolled casually from the bedroom into the living room, ignoring his impatient insistence as I made my way to the fridge for a bottle of water.

"You're not wearing that, are you?" he asked, mouth agape. Looking at me like I was all wrong.

I quickly passed my eyes over my black silk sliplike skirt and my peasant blouse. "What's wrong with my clothes?"

"You look like a hippie whore."

"What?" I asked, outrage snapping the "t" into its own syllable.

"That outfit is all wrong. You'll stick out like a sore thumb."

"I'm not trying to fit in. Remember, I'm not Greek, despite my AKA looks. Besides, I'm working," I said, gathering my camera bag.

"Shanna, I'm introducing you to the mayor today."

"I already met him."

"Yeah, but not as my woman."

"What difference does it make?" I huffed.

"It makes all the difference in the world. Go put on something else, and hurry," he ordered.

"I'm doing no such thing."

"Look, Shanna," he said, his voice quivering with anger. "I don't have time to play with you. Now go take that shit off and put on something decent. Wear the suit that you wore to the funeral. Why you trying to fuckin' embarrass me with this bullshit?"

"This isn't about you."

"God damn it, yes it is," he fumed, starting toward me.

My mind flashed back, dredging up the image of my mother cowering under my father's tight grasp. Tears filled my eyes as I replayed her frightened whisper. "Where's Shanna?"

His hands were on my arms, pressing into my flesh until it turned bright red in his grasp. My body was limp as he yanked me toward him. Anger registered in his eyes, silently warning me to heed his words. He pushed me away, and I stumbled backward moving unseeing toward the bedroom. I tumbled inside the door, and my hands shook as I frantically searched the closet for the black linen suit that I had worn to my grandmother's funeral. I fumbled as I removed the skirt and blouse, haphazardly pulling on the long black linen skirt and matching jacket. Hurrying back into the living room, I found Lionel standing with his hand on the doorknob, looking irritated while checking the time on his watch. He snarled at me as I scampered to pick up my camera bag, and together we headed outside into the oppressive July heat.

i still hear them

Sometimes when it's quiet, or not so quiet, when it's calm, or when it's stormy, when I'm at rest, or when I'm active, I still hear them.

Their voices are small, almost inaudible at first, and they sound joyful like kids in a playground. The voices escalate, growing louder, and they seem to be fighting for my attention. Then they become thunderous, almost deafening, and the words, they are like stones being hurled at me, breaking my skin, exposing my vulnerable flesh, and shaking my core.

"halfrican"

"mutt"

"half-breed"

"zebra"

"oreo"

"whigger"

"white girl"

"nigger bitch"

"Halfrican!"

"Mutt!"

"Half-breed!"

"Zebra!"

"Oreo!"

"Whigger!"

"White girl!"

"Nigger bitch!"

"HALFRICAN!"

"MUTT!"

"HALF-BREED!"

"ZEBRA!"

"OREO!"

"WHIGGER!"

"WHITE GIRL!"

"NIGGER BITCH!"

They chant it like a nursery rhyme, and I try to counter it with my own weak one.

"Sticks and stones may break my bones, but words can . . . hurt me forever."

developing

Standing in my darkroom, I swished the photography paper around in the solution, tongs moving from right to left. As always I was holding my breath, waiting for the image to take shape. When the white paper began to turn gray, I exhaled and mentally nursed the image along. Pulling the photograph from the liquid, I took it to my makeshift clothesline and clipped it on the white border, letting the liquid drip onto the floor. Methodically I moved, developing picture after picture, trying not to study the content of the photos, merely scanning each one to make sure I had given it enough time to set. The clothesline filled with drying pictures, I made my way through the layers of black fabric draped inside of the room to block the light that would enter when I opened the door.

In the living room I grabbed the keys and my bag, heading to the jeep. With shades perched on my nose, I glided the truck out of the enclosed gate and into traffic heading to work at The Gallery. I had increased my summer hours at the cheesy department store, which insured more money for the summer, but the work felt like it was smothering me, constricting my breathing as I snapped the staged photos. I saw how the people slapped fake, temporary smiles on their faces, and the smiles acted like masks, momentarily covering up whatever problems or difficulties were looming over their lives. I wasn't as forgiving.

Lionel had hurt me. It wasn't that my existence had been buttery and he had been the warm jagged knife cutting the meat from my life. I had issues, and I knew it, but my issues didn't creep their way into his reality, edging in on him. I simply was. I wasn't imposing, and I didn't hurt anyone. Yet people were always hurting me. Taunting me, deserting me, ignoring me, and crushing me.

I was a dandelion puff, a hybrid that had been around forever. Some saw the beauty in me and stooped quietly to admire my innocence. Others saw the potential of what I could do for them, so they uprooted me, seeking to shape me around their needs. They blew at my head, scattering my hair from the roots, changing me to suit them. Yet still others saw me as something that was unworthy and needed to be erased. Yanked out and discarded because I did not and could not serve any practical purpose. I was nothing more than a weed, and weeds need not exist. Lionel's thinking placed me squarely in category two. I was to be what he needed me to be, just like my mother was supposed to be the symbol of my father's arrival. Not like Bobby McFerrin's artistic, free-spirited love. More like O. J.'s obsessive white girl adoration. A smiling trophy. A plaque. A treasure to be ogled. That was it. Nothing more. I knew that I could be no one's trophy. And I had to find a way to break free before Lionel suffocated me.

That evening I returned home and went to my darkroom to examine my photos before writing captions on the ones from the mayor's reception and giving subtitles to the shots of Lionel's northbound and southbound runs.

I had taken a series of Lionel approaching as I stood on the sidewalk facing him. He looked like he was running toward me, ready to leap from the page, and it momentarily scared me. His lean muscled flesh was sculpted beneath his plain white tank top and shorts. He looked latently powerful in the picture, and that, too, scared me. Anguish was branded on his face as he stared straight ahead. To his left, cars dotted the curb intermittently like witches' teeth, and to his right, slabs of concrete forming three-stepped front stoops jutted out. Some were littered with discarded forty-ounce bottles of malt liquor, their brown heads peeking from the tops of rumpled tan paper bags. Other stoops were decorated with beautiful souls trapped inside of hopeless people.

On one stoop sat a young brown woman. Dolled up, she wore big earrings and high heels. Her dark hair was cut in layers and shaped into a soft Halle Berry taper. Her bloated body was mismatched with her thin arms, which were extended toward Lionel. In her hands, she offered him a small child who also reached toward the man who was running past with anguish engraved on his face, and his hands were clenched in tight balls.

my trek

I found my way back to the block with ease. And the small child, a boy, playing with pebbles that he hid in a can and shook noisily, indicated that this was his house. I sat on the steps adjacent to the house, waiting. I knew that the bloated woman would come to the door to check on the bronze-colored child. I knew that she would see me and glare at me across the street. I knew that she would go back into the house, mumbling curses, asking herself rhetorically why I had brought my high yellow ass around there in the first place. I knew that she would storm back out the door and scoop up her child, shooting dagger eyes at me all the while. I knew that she would stare confrontationally at me, half-daring me to speak, half-hoping that I wouldn't say a word. I knew that she would not return my wave, and as I approached, she would stare at me, a sham of bitter defiance in her dark eyes. I knew that she would use the child as a buffering shield between us, his body the precise median shade between her own and Lionel's. And I knew that she would let him slide from her hip, sinking to the ground where he would look from woman to woman, eyes questioning but mouth too young to formulate the words behind the questions. And I knew that he would return to his pebble and can game, playing innocently, a cherub trapped in hell. And I knew that she would lead me into the rickety rented house where she would rant and rave about the promises that he had spoken but not honored. I knew that her voice would go high as the tears choked her story out of her. I knew that her body would ripple as the tears broke forth, her resolve a weak dam that buckled under my hazel eyes. I knew that, childlike, she would allow me to lead her to the worn-out couch where her body would continue to quake, shaking loose tears from my own eyes. I knew that images of high yellow women of privilege, athletes' wives, musicians' wives, politicians' wives, and actors' wives would dance in her eyes. And I knew that she would look at me imagining millions of ways to degrade me inside of the rented house in the middle of the crumbling neighborhood while the child that he refused, and would continue to refuse, played with pebbles and a can on the sidewalk, the same sidewalk that would eventually drink up the child's blood as he struggled to be a man born into a manless house.

cooling

I remembered the heat I had felt from him the first time I saw him. It had been intense, as if a light was burning from within, emitting a radiant glow that screamed for my attention. And I had seen the spark, drawn to the glow like a moth to a flame, never knowing that death lay within the fire.

The fire had raged on, burning brightly within me, the always loving moth, worshiping it like an idol. But I had gotten too close. I had gone through the flame, and it had singed my wings. A little longer in the fire and I wouldn't have been able to get away. And as I pulled out, licking my wounds, trying to nurse myself because no one else would or could, I saw carcasses around me of those who had been burned before me. They were less outwardly majestic, but still beautiful because they were. They simply were. But even my perceived beauty could not keep me from getting scorched.

So I set my mind on withdrawing, on getting away from the thing that had the power to hurt, and as I moved away from the light, I moved away from the heat as well, for fire can burn only those close to it. But once away, I recognize it for what it is, a simple spark no greater than any others.

And that knowledge cools me.

peace

He arrived in town on the Friday before the Greek Picnic, the annual event during which Philadelphia plays host to thousands of college students from across the country. The event used to be solely for those students who had pledged membership to one of the nine historically black fraternities and sororities in the Pan-Hellenic Council, but in recent years, non-Greeks and then noncollege students converged on the city. In the past year or two, high school students had stormed the Belmont Plateau as well, girls vying for the attention of the older guys by wearing strips of fabric they called clothes while the young bucks, armed with video cameras to capture and preserve the hedonistic display, dared girls to reveal body parts. Only the young girls did, though, giggling all the way.

Peace rang the doorbell in the early afternoon, smiling broadly when I answered the door.

"What's up, Shanna?" he said, swaggering in.

"Hey, Peace," I said, ushering him into the living room.

"They don't grow women like you up in Brick City," he commented, moving toward the kitchen table, which was cluttered with pictures I had taken of Lionel, of Virginia, and of natural settings throughout Fairmount Park. Peace lingered over the nature shots.

"You take good pictures," he said. "I'm feeling these flicks of trees and water and shit."

"Come look at this," I said leading him into the bedroom and gesturing toward the wall where the impressive shot of the trees was stretched across the canvas hanging on the wall.

"That's tight. You know you've got to hook a brother up, right?" Peace inquired, patting me on the back.

"What dorm do you know that has this kind of wall space?"

"You could do a little one for me," he said.

"Maybe," I responded noncommittally, leading him from the room.

I moved toward the kitchen where I stood at the kitchen sink, beginning to rinse off dishes before loading them into the dishwasher. "Lionel won't be here for another three hours or so," I offered, hating the feeling of the wet glass under my fingers.

"How shall we pass the time?" he mused.

He didn't know what he was asking. At that moment I craved nothing more than to feel his honey-colored, sun-kissed skin against mine, undiluted, unpretentious, rugged soul rocking me from the inside out. The cool ball in my belly would allow me to acquiesce even though the light in my head was flashing a yellow warning signal. I knew that it wouldn't be right for me to cross this line with Peace, but neither were a lot of other things. Like planting seeds you didn't intend to water. Like invading space without a question. Like planning to recast me into the image that best suited him. Like putting fear in my heart in my own home.

"Why are you called Peace?" I asked, stalling for time while I worked on clearing the sink.

"My first name is British and it begins with a P, and my last name is German and it begins with an S. Meanwhile I'm black as night."

"Sounds confusing," I chuckled.

"That's the only thing about me that is conflicted," he said, moving toward me. "Everything else about me is straight up. You know?" he asked rhetorically, pressing his erection against my behind.

"Yeah, straight up," I murmured breathily, feeling the ball of ice in my stomach begin to thaw, sending droplets of water down into my vagina.

"So why did you choose 'Peace' instead of 'Pest' or something else," I asked, feeling the air being sucked out of the room.

"Because there's a war inside of all of us. Right. Wrong. Good. Evil. Black. White. This is the equalizer. The neutralizer. The peacemaker. How do you like?" he asked with one arm wrapped around my stomach and the other removing the glass from my hand. He dropped it in the sink where it shattered. And I didn't care.

"Hard," I responded.

"Then hard it is," he said, biting my shoulder.

As I felt his teeth press into my flesh, I groaned masochistically. He pinched my nipple through my shirt, and I winced in pained pleasure, reveling in the hurt that I deserved for being stupid enough to allow Lionel into my heart and home. His pressing his teeth into my cursed, cream skin was an extension of my self-mutilation. And I wanted him to rip me to shreds.

"Go to the bedroom," he ordered through his succulent lips, picking up a large shard of glass.

I complied wordlessly, loving the frenzy he was creating in me.

In the bedroom, I leaned against the wall next to the trees, my body quivering with anticipation. He came in and looked at me, his lusty brown eyes roaming over my body and feeling like hot pin-pricks. I could see that he was as hungry as I was, and I wouldn't deny him.

Using the glass, he slit the top of my shirt, making a small incision between my breasts and pressing the smooth but sharp edge into my skin. I flinched as I felt the pressure of the glass against my flesh. He searched my face for signs of real fear, and seeing none, he continued tracing it across my heaving chest. He put the glass between my teeth, freeing up his hands to rip the fabric of my tank top open. He found my creamy breasts unbridled by a bra, jiggling slightly as my body quivered. He cupped my mounds roughly, smashing my erect, raisinlike nipples between his lips, and the agony I felt was so satisfying that I felt a guttural rumble inside me.

Peace clasped my wrists together in his strong hands, and he raised them, pinning them to the wall above my head. He took in my body, beginning first with my feet. His eyes climbed up my shins, stopping at the black silk slipskirt that Lionel hated. Peace rubbed the petal-smooth material between his fingers and smiled, kneeling to bury his face in the softness.

"What's that I smell?" he said, his nose pressed into my crotch. He rubbed his face all around, releasing my hands, freeing them to wander through the tight curls of his hair. "Is that the scent of wet pussy?"

"Mm-hmm," I mumbled.

"Whose is it?" he asked, still inhaling my aroma.

"It's yours now," I whispered, speaking around the glass in my teeth.

"Say it again," he commanded.

"It's yours now," I repeated, heartened by my deception and not caring if my mouth was cut by the glass.

He slid the skirt from my hips, feeling the ripe fullness of them. He took the glass from my mouth and cut the skimpy strips of my thong. My panties fell to the floor in a tattered heap, and he dropped the shard of glass on top of them.

Clasping my hands over my head again, Peace resumed his visual body search, smiling at my shaved vagina before continuing to scan my stomach then my breasts. He stopped when he saw the scarred flesh of my inner arms near my breasts.

"Oh, baby," he mumbled tenderly, kissing the scars, using his tongue to trace the flesh that had been punctured and puckered by my sewing needle, and I cried. He licked my tears before pressing his mouth to mine, offering me my salty tears to swallow.

I unbuckled his pants and slid them down, fingering a scar on the lower part of his stomach. His body pressed against mine, his muscled flesh firm and unyielding against my softness.

"Condom," I whispered, nodding toward the dresser where they lay exposed because Lionel never put anything away.

After sliding it on, he made slow gyrations with his hips, rendering me weak. I lifted my legs around his waist, locking my ankles firmly and preparing for what I knew would be the ride of my life.

"Do it to me hard," I reminded him because I deserved the roughness.

His penis became a sword that he rammed into me, jabbing at my walls with ferocity. As he moved in and out, he thrust my body against the hard wall, and the trees vibrated in synchronicity. Before we could settle into a routine, he loosened my legs, dropping them to the floor and mercilessly withdrawing from within me.

Turning me around, he plunged in from behind, fortifying himself against the wall with one hand and savagely yanking my hair with the other. The roughness thrilled me, and with my arms supporting me against the wall, I panted with ecstasy. He ravaged me like a lusty pirate, his thickness diving in and out, stealing my treasure while simultaneously giving me pleasure. He let go of my hair and slapped my ass roughly, redeeming me each time his hand connected with my skin.

Again he turned me, alternately kissing, biting, and sucking my lips. He lowered our bodies to the floor, pulling me on top where I straddled his lean hips. I rode the crest of his body, sweat coursing down my face and neck, slowing to a trickle on my breastbone before collecting with other droplets and racing down my stomach, across my navel, and down toward my womanly folds. He used his thumb to trace the path of my sweat, finally nestling it under my throbbing clit. As we rocked rhythmically, I felt as if a flint had been lit deep within my gut. With every delicious stroke the fire grew in intensity, melting the remnants of the ice ball in my stomach. The ice turned to water that simmered, then bubbled within me. I clutched his shoulders as I felt the water begin to boil.

"Say you love me, Shanna," he commanded.

Confusion registered on my face, but I couldn't stop the ride.

"Say it, Shanna, or I'll stop right now."

"Don't stop," I panted, pleading.

"Well, say it. Tell me, damn it," he ordered, slowing his undulations.

Confusion subsided, and lust turned to love, and as the words formed on my tongue, I could feel the click of the boil.

"I love you, Peace. I love you, Peace."

The words flew from my mouth as the orgasm rocked my core.

My tightening walls pulled him over the edge as he exploded with ardent fervor. His hips thrust forward, and he grabbed my waist, holding me until our quaking ceased. He didn't withdraw until I moved first.

I curled inside of him, a ball in his concave body, and I fell into a sound sleep.

introductions iii

It wasn't enough that I had fucked Peace. It wasn't enough that I had given comfort to the woman and child Lionel had abandoned on his climb toward upward mobility. I needed to see him down. I needed to see him damaged, ruined, for what he was doing to me.

The opportunity came easier than I expected. I was cooking dinner one evening while Bob Marley serenaded me. The whiskey I was gulping mellowed me from a weary day, and when Lionel came in, he leaned against the counter watching me as I harmonized with Bob.

"You look like you're having fun," he said.

I simply nodded, swallowing the liquor that burned my throat in its descent. I passed the glass to him while I tasted the curried chicken I was cooking. Out of the corner of my eye I saw him examining it, swirling it, smelling it. Then he lifted it easily to his mouth, coughing after it went down. I refilled the glass, took it from him, and swallowed again, offering him a challenge. He imitated me, sucking it up like a baby sucks milk, like it was second nature, like it was in his blood. Then I thought about it. The yearning for alcohol was in his blood, courtesy of his father.

The next morning the smell of burned curried chicken and vomit mingled in the air, producing a stink that sank into Lionel's bones. He remembered the promise that he'd made to himself that he would never drink because of the destruction it had wrought upon his father, and he laughed. He laughed because he'd believed that he could outrun his genes and dodge fate. He'd believed that he could transcend his father's demon, but in one night he'd been sucked back in. And blood never forgets its innate desire.

He drank with a discipline that supplanted his runner's constitution, and as he plunged into the abyss, my own footing became less sure. I was destroying him, and my heart hurt. He ventured back to the badlands where his ambition had transformed him into a legend. When they saw him stumble back, not to uplift but to be lifted up, their hopes were dashed. Those who cared chastised themselves for putting their faith in a man, for he had let them down.

His downward spiral was swift. Late August found him no longer working but attending classes sporadically. September found him barely attending classes and barely bathing. October found him belligerently barking out demands when he made his way to the apartment after a long drinking binge. Having lost his key, he'd bang on the door, kicking it and screaming loudly until I opened it and he fell into a liquor-induced slumber.

Guilt consumed me by November, and I did everything I could to ease the pain that I had caused. Lionel was in too deep to crawl out on his own. His body was programmed not to stop. And the knowledge that I had set the ball in motion ate away at me.

I was rushing home to him one rainy evening in November, thinking that I was surely going to hell. At least I would finally get the chance to meet my grandmother, I mused, as I approached the intersection at Broad and Girard. In my frenzy I sped toward the intersection not noticing the flashing red lights in the intersection. By the time I saw the other car, it was inches from the passenger side. It slammed into me, throwing me through the doorless opening and out into the street where I lay, hearing the frantic voices circling over my head.

part three

white

broken

My body seemed like a jigsaw puzzle whose pieces had to be gently put back together. One cracked pelvis, two broken legs, a concussion, three broken ribs, one broken arm, one busted lip, and two black eyes. I was a mess. And the person who the police and paramedics called was the last person I wanted to see.

When she'd stood weeping in the doorway of my hospital room, she wasn't sure what my reaction to her would be. A decade had passed, and I'd grown into a woman without her. And I'd needed her, more than she could ever know.

I turned to look at her, and the anger that I'd had for her spilled down my cheek. I'd wailed, trying to scream away the pain that had been trapped in me, but I'd succeeded only in having two orderlies escort her from my room.

Every day, she came back, and I cried more. It took six days to destroy the pain that had taken years to be built. And on the seventh day, I sat quietly as she entered. And I waited.

Over the ensuing months, as I learned to walk again, and live again, and love again, she was my biggest cheerleader. She had proven herself when she rushed to the hospital, and when I allowed her to, she cradled my head and clutched my hand as if she were fighting for her own life. Although I didn't want to trust her, my heart needed me to so that I could forgive. And grow. And move on.

rebirth

Nine months, she gave me. Nine months to rehabilitate my body. Nine months to fix my mind. Nine months to heal my soul. Nine months to learn to live again for the very first time.

Locked behind the walls of the Main Line castle, my mother nourished me, satiating my hunger for knowledge. She bathed me in her birthing water, sprinkled me with the powder of her love, wrapped me in the warmth of tenderness, and fattened me with breast milk oozing with security. I was her baby again, solely at her mercy. The steps I took delighted her, and she was enraptured by my first sensible utterances. She was determined to love me back to health.

Locked behind the walls of the Main Line estate, we were free of probing questions and accusing stares. Free of the cowering stances under which we bent to the wills of others. The bending had been difficult, more life threatening than a break. A break is quick and merciful. The thing is left to rot in peace, never having to fix itself for the eyes and questions of others. Never having to explain its irregularities. It's simply broken, and people can weep if they will. But the constant bending is hard. The bender creates new and torturous ways to torment. New ways to test the limits, never once stopping to hear the quiet scream pressing forth from the soul of the thing. But there in the Main Line castle, my mother and I, two bent things, screamed our way back to sanity.

Locked behind the walls of the Main Line castle, my mother told me her stories of love and longing and loss. Of privilege and power and pain. Of chaos and cowering and crying. Of greed and gravity and guilt. Of happiness and hurt and hate. She doled out the tales with as much objectivity as the teller can have, and she left me with those swirling molecules, urging me to give them shape.

Nine months of hoping and hearing, and when she emerged from behind the walls of the Main Line castle bearing me, her beautiful bundle, I had been reborn.

telling it

My mother was no longer a victim, and that freedom radiated from her eyes. She moved with ease through stiff crowds at parties we attended, her grace making their rigidity even more pronounced. Her smile was the garnish on the plate, making an already beautiful dish that much prettier. Although she was fair from head to toe, the other women paled in comparison to her, for she was a lovely tigress who had ventured from the fold, daring to live. She had stepped outside the box, crossing the line of the Main Line and tasting the forbidden fruit. She had known love, had lived with loss, while those shadows of women had chosen to live in safety. The living had cost her, but the end result was beautiful, for she had me. And I was worth every tear, she said.

"I was, of course, thrilled when I brought you home from Chestnut Hill Hospital. You were gorgeous even then, and people always gathered around to ogle you. You could draw a crowd even then."

"Yeess," she sighed smiling, continuing to reflect on my infancy. "The Main Line thing to do would have been to bring in a European au pair, preferably French. The Chestnut Hill thing to do would have been to hire a black nanny. I didn't want that, though. Looking up into her face and seeing your father daily would have made you think I was an outsider, and I refused to feel that way with my child. I made you my life. Anything Shanna wanted, Shanna got. Nothing was too much. Nothing impossible. Nothing except getting your father to hold you.

"At first I thought it was just male nerves, you know. You were so small, and I figured that he was afraid that he would hurt you. But that wasn't it. I pressed you on him, but he just gave you back to me. One day when he was off from work, I told him that I needed to make a quick run, and that he needed to keep an eye on you until I got back. You were in your carryall bassinet-like thing, so it wasn't like he had to hold you in his arms. Before he could protest, I was out the door. I rode to the store and picked up something I didn't need, hoping to get him to open up and accept you.

"When I got home, you both were exactly where I had left you. You were crying, and your little face was all red. I felt that mother's guilt, and I rushed over to pick you up. I ignored him while I was shushing you, but as soon as you quieted, I turned to him. I remember that he was just looking at the floor like there was no one there. I said, 'The baby was crying.' He just looked at me really slowly, and he said simply, 'I didn't want a baby.' I launched into a whining fit about responsibility and pitching in and a bunch of other unrelated stuff, and when I finished, he was still looking at me, this maniac holding a baby. And he said simply, 'Elizabeth, I'm not whole. I'm not what a baby needs.'

"I went overboard, gushing about what a wonderful father he would be once he got the hang of it and how all new parents were nervous, but he just had to go with the flow. I said a lot of things that afternoon, but I missed hearing what I was supposed to hear. He'd said that he wasn't whole, but I'd pushed him into doing something he had no desire to do. And there was no turning back. I had gotten my way, and I hadn't regretted it, but I hadn't stopped to listen to him. From that moment, I knew that I would have to be your all. You can see what a miserable job I did with that."

She had stopped talking, her eyes following a rabbit that was hopping across the yard.

"I'm okay," I said, trying to reassure her.

"Now," she responded, swallowing soberly.

focusing

At first I had trouble picking up the camera again. I hadn't used it in a while, especially since I hadn't worked since my accident. Acidic guilt ate away at my psyche every time I thought about holding that which had been an extension of me for years. It had been the truth serum I used to make sense of the world, capturing people midstream in a way that made them flat, one-dimensional creatures devoid of follow-through. Then I realized that it was no truth serum. The camera served only to distance me from my subject and my subjects from the world. Sometimes the objectification made them seem larger than life if they were moneyed or noble or even tragically distraught. They were like visual martyrs, never changing, never blooming, never evolving. Like sex without orgasm. Unfinished yet somehow vaguely fulfilling for its temporary closeness. But the lover never climaxes, so the experience is futile. Like a cute, not funny, joke. A mediocre meal. A sketch of a painting to be done.

The real art was in capturing the subject in a way that made it seem as though a story were being told. I told myself that if I could create a visual essay, then maybe I could pick up the camera again with renewed confidence and steady focus.

revealing

"Your father always was a man of few words," my mother said as we lounged on the chaises on the stone patio. Above us, thick, unruly ivy wove its way through the wooden beams that formed a skeleton of an awning.

"He had to say something to you at some time," I offered.

"He communicated with his heart, but I couldn't hear it," she mumbled, taking a swig of her lemony water, which had been lemonade when we came out here after dinner.

I waited for her to talk, to fill in the gaps of the picture of my father in her low, steady way.

"When I met him, he was working in stock at Saks. I was there with one of my girlfriends from Brown who was spending Christmas break with me. She was a really sweet girl from New York named Shoshanna. Her parents had reared her on healthy doses of unity, equality, and love for humanity. She was so different from my Main Line pals, who, though never overtly racist because that would be unmannerly and rude, believed that separate had been equal and there was no need to confuse matters.

"Well, Shoshanna and I trotted around the store, not looking for anything in particular but trying on everything in sight. My mother would have killed me if she'd seen be behaving so commonly, but I was with my buddy Shoshanna, so I didn't care. She had this dark mane that was brimming with thick lustrous curls. She had me try to iron it once at school, but it was so humid that day that as soon as we stepped outside, it started rising up, returning to its natural puff. She looked like Juan from *Welcome Back Kotter.*

"Well anyway, this day we started goofing around in hats, trying them on for fun. She was cracking me up with her impersonations of ladies-who-lunch, who actually were a part of my mother's circle, and this saleswoman came over to tell us to settle down. Shoshanna didn't like her tone, and she mouthed off to her. When she finished, the woman looked at her and said, 'Typical.' Shoshanna just lost it. She was on fire.

" 'Typical of what?' she said. 'Typical of short people? Typical of thin people? What? Typical of curly-haired people?'

"She kept firing at her, and the woman looked scared. She started to walk away, but Shoshanna kept following her, still hammering away. I followed her to make sure that she didn't take a swing at the woman, who, by now, was scared out of her wits.

"Well, she chased the poor woman into one of the stockrooms, still whaling on her. The woman called security from a phone in the back, and I could hear the coded bells going off. We didn't want to go back into the store and run into danger, but we didn't know where to go. Just then your father appeared like a knight out of nowhere, and Shoshanna asked him for help. He ushered us out the door to the loading dock, and we took off without even saying thank you.

"The next day we drove back to the store. I made Shoshanna promise to stay in the car before we drove around to the loading dock looking for him. He had saved me some serious embarrassment, and I had a little thank you gift for him. He smiled when he saw us, calling us the Main Line rebels. Then I gave him the gift. It was a pot of gooseberry jam and scones from Biba's Boulangerie. Boy, did he laugh. I asked him what was so funny, and he said that the gift was very Main Line. I let Shoshanna get out of the car to thank him personally. He said that he was about to go on a coffee break, and he wondered if we wanted to hang around. We spent the next half hour on the loading dock drinking coffee from his thermos and eating gooseberry jam on scones. I'm sure that we were a sight, hanging on a loading dock in the dead of winter."

She stopped talking and smiled at the invisible image. I didn't coax her because it wasn't in her nature to be rushed. Besides, I was trying to conjure an image of my father as a young man, standing with two white women outside on a bitter Philadelphia December day in 1968. His historical sense of the past would have told him not to even speak to the white women because that could equal trouble. WASP or Jew, a black man wouldn't distinguish because white was still white and black was still black. Shoshanna with her civil rights sensibilities might have viewed him as a cause, but my mother would have simply viewed him as a man. A man darker than she was used to, but a man no less. And a man needs a woman.

"We went to see him every day during Christmas break. It became one of our things to do. Running on Kelly Drive, volunteering for the lunch shift at the homeless shelter, showering and getting dressed, going for facials, manicures, pedicures, or massages at the spa, taking a coffee break at Saks, going to a movie, attending a holiday party of a family friend.

"He kissed me before I left for the spring semester, and I loved the feel of his lips on mine. I dreamed about it for weeks. I gave him my number at school, and we talked regularly for months. Well, he mostly listened. We met in New York on some weekends, and . . . we

debut

...her's friend Graham was having a party to celebrate the ...th anniversary of his magazine. Mom thought that it would ...onderful opportunity for me to get out and meet some peo- ...'Perhaps even jump-start your photography career," she said. ...I wasn't sure I was ready to do that yet. She sensed my hesitation ...d said, "Even if you don't plan to do that, it can't hurt you to get ...ut for a few hours."

So a half hour after the official start time of the party, we rolled into the Lanning Theater, an old cabaret house that had recently been refurbished. We both wore white pantsuits and stunning amber jewelry the same shade as my hair. Looking in the mirror of the ladies' room, I felt almost pretty despite the ugliness lurking beneath my skin. Lord knows, my mother was doing everything in her power to nurture me, but sometimes I still felt that old emptiness.

All night she made introductions, showing me off like a prized possession, but I still felt lowly. I smiled politely while admiring the ease with which my mother moved in this world. I remembered how uncomfortable she had seemed all those years ago when she took me to lunch that afternoon. Now I realized that the discomfort was

had a great time. Everything was so new to him, and I loved being the one to show it to him. It was beautiful and innocent and sweet. We eloped that summer after I graduated. Things were rocky with my parents when we got married, but with us, life was good for a while."

I noted the pause in her narrative, and I filled in the next sentence for myself. Without her saying it, I knew that the unspoken line was, "Until you were born." Oddly, I wasn't saddened by the thought. It just was, and no tears could change that.

"I named you after Shoshanna because I wanted you to have her spirit. She was a fighter then, and she still is. She's an attorney now also. I've never known anyone braver, who'd sacrifice herself for someone she cared about. Until you."

She squeezed my hand, and I swallowed hard remembering Lionel and wondering where he was.

daddy

"Shanna, I'm moving back to Virginia," my father said.

I had known that this was coming since our trip there for my grandmother's funeral. He had so many holes in him, and Hampton seemed to be the only place where he had felt some semblance of being filled. His roots were there, and that was where he needed to be, with his flesh, and his people. I knew what it was to be disconnected, and I wouldn't wish that on anyone. I gave him my blessing, knowing that he didn't need it. Yet somewhere inside, I knew he wanted it. That's why he had gone out on a limb and called me at my mother's house.

"When are you leaving?"

"Two weeks. The house is already sold, so you'll need to get anything that you want from here."

I couldn't think of anything from there that I needed. I had been out of the house for almost three years, and if I hadn't used something in that time, chances are that I wouldn't miss it. The stuff that mattered to me had been moved to my apartment, and my mother brought it all to her house after she'd gone to Northern Liberties to clean out my place.

"Dad, I don't think that there's anything there that I need," I said.

As soon as I spoke the w
there for seventeen ye
from the time spent the

"Okay, then," he was sa

"I'll come look anyway,
wanted to see him again, too, b
tween us. I knew that I needed to
help you pack, too," I offered lamely.

"Fine," he said flatly.

"I'll be over in a few days."

"Mm-hmm."

"See ya."

"Bye."

born of the collision of both of her worlds. She, of course, had known how to behave in both worlds separately, but when they were thrown together and personified in me, her daughter, the equation became a little more tricky. Somewhere, somehow she had learned that she couldn't escape what she was. She was privileged through no doing of her own, and guilt, though omnipresent, was pointless. Just be, she finally seemed to say to herself. And now she was inviting me in, praying that I would fit with her.

"Shanna, meet Ricki and Leonard Tavian. They own that great secluded restaurant on the waterfront in Manayunk and a slew of others up and down Germantown Avenue and Main Street."

"Honey, this is Midge Shaunessy. She owns the jewelry store on the corner of Montgomery and Cranberry."

"Dear, I've known this lady for over half of my life. Ginger, you must meet my gorgeous daughter Shanna. Shanna, Ginger owns the bottling plant just south of the city."

My mother was in her element, and she was the toast of the town. Liddy, they called her, greeting her easily like she had never left the fold. And she was happy here.

"Come, Shanna. I want you to meet my dear old friend Graham England. Graham and I go way back to our youth. He attended the Shipley School, which was right next door to the Baldwin School, which, of course, I attended," my mother explained. "Graham, this is my beautiful daughter Shanna."

We shook hands and uttered niceties while my mother chattered on about my being a photographer.

"Who have you worked for?"

"I've done some work with the *Herald* and a few other publications," I responded, not expecting him to recognize the name of the black periodical.

"Oh, yes. I know Monty Goode very well. We golf once a month," he said.

"He's a great guy," I said, masking my surprise.

"He is. I'm sure he's not paying you what you're worth, the cheap bastard," Graham laughed good-naturedly.

"I . . . I haven't done anything for him for a while," I mumbled.

"Doesn't matter. He's still cheap. But he's good. He runs a quality paper, and if you're good enough for him . . . well, I trust him. Why don't you give me a call? Your mother has my home number. I'd like to see your portfolio."

"Okay, Mr. England. I'll . . ."

"Graham," he interjected.

"Okay, Graham. I'll be sure to call."

He squeezed my hand and moved off into another circle of people congratulating him on making the twenty-year mark.

"Welcome to your world," my mother said grinning.

I couldn't help but smile back.

when you were born

"Pregnancy is such a beautiful thing. When you were born, I realized that I had been readying my body for you all my life. It was a relatively easy pregnancy, but delivery, of course, was more difficult, you know. Like squeezing a honeydew out of one's crotch. People always say that when you look at your newborn child, you forget all of the pain that you endured. That's an absolute lie. You remember it all, especially on those nights when the baby just won't stop crying. However, what you come to realize is that giving birth is your only chance to assist God in a miracle. So you quit your complaining and gloss over the rough memories.

"I had put on a substantial amount of weight when I was carrying you. This was before the days when pregnant women bared their balloon bellies like they do now. We all wore tents, and we looked beautiful. My arms had gotten heavy, and I refused to go out in public in anything that came above the elbow. My legs looked like pork sausages, but I didn't care about that so much because people rarely looked that low. Their eyes always came to rest on my stomach, so no one saw my legs besides your father and the doctor parade that marched through every time I was at the ob/gyn. The doctors were sympathetic because they were used to seeing bloated women.

"After you were born, I pretty much dropped back down to my regular size instantly. I was still puffy around the middle, though, and my breasts were huge. I had a favorite nightgown that I'd wear. Shoshanna had sent it to me after I told her the good news, and I thought it was so pretty. It gave both you and your father easy access, so it was ideal. It was silvery green, and it had these thin spaghetti straps. The front had lacy cut-outs, and there were high splits on the sides.

"One night, your father said, 'That nightgown is too hot.' I waited for an explanation because I was wondering why he was worried about the temperature of my gown. It didn't make any sense, so I ignored it. The next night he said, 'That thing is too tight. Why are you always wearing that?' I was floored. Here, it was the only thing that I felt comfortable in, and I thought it was mildly sexy, and here he was complaining about it. So the next day while he was at work, I threw it in the garbage, kind of like a subtle protest of acquiescence. I was so hurt, and he never knew it. I just swallowed it down, and it was bitter. But swallowing down the hurt got easier as time went on. The thing that you never know, though, is that every time you swallow, you get a little fuller. And then one day, you have to excuse yourself from the table because you can't take another bite."

looking for lionel 1

Guilt about Lionel crowded my dreams more and more until it began to shake me awake, and there in the nighttime stillness behind the walls of the Main Line castle, I whispered the words over and over until the tears streamed down my cheeks.

"I broke a man. I broke a man," I would say, punishing myself for the torture I had thrust upon him.

Because of me, two women in two North Philadelphia hovels felt an emptiness matched only by the Grand Canyon. Because of me, another black boy would be robbed of the chance to know his father the way he should. He would know him through angry utterances hissed through the clenched teeth of his mother. They would be of the "Your-daddy-wasn't-shit" variety. And I would forever be the "white girl" who had turned him out.

I couldn't be that. It hurt too much. So there in the nighttime stillness, I planned to find the pictures of Lionel running past them on one of his remembering journeys. And I would put them in an envelope. And I would write a note that read, "He loved you." And I would count out several large bills. And I would stuff it and the note into a smaller envelope. And I would drive it to her house under the cover of night. And I would pray that she would find it in her heart to forgive me.

guilty pleasure

"Another thing Shoshanna said when I broke the news of our marriage was that I should always have a guilty pleasure that I unpacked and indulged in when times got rough," my mother confided as we sat in our usual place on the stone patio one evening.

"I didn't know what she'd meant initially. Money certainly wasn't an issue, and your father certainly seemed calm and reasonable. I wanted to press her to explain, but she told me it wasn't her place, and that if I were meant to drink from that cup, then I'd taste it sooner or later. But sooner came too soon.

"The signs were always there, but I didn't know how to confront them. Truthfully, I didn't even know if it was my place. Sounds crazy, I know, but your father was an island of one. Solitary and elusive. I have the feeling that if I ever got up the courage to ask him, he would've answered me honestly, but I had been stripped of my courage. So when the strange hairs and strange scents appeared, I was too cowardly to say a word. It wasn't regular, just every so often, I reasoned with myself. I always knew when it was happening. Wives always know. They just don't want to admit it.

"So I learned what Shoshanna meant, and I found my own guilty pleasure. He was your pediatrician, Dr. David Hunter. I'd call him every time I heard you sniffle. I hoped that he'd chalk it up to new mother nerves, but it was more. He saved me with his kindness. He always took my calls, and for that I found simple ways to thank him. A nice winter scarf. Supple leather driving gloves. Expensive pens. He was kind enough to indulge me, and he accepted the gifts with grace, and that was all I needed. Those gifts and my fantasies of him.

"Then, I had a birthday party for you at the house one year."

My mother breathed deeply, knowing that I needed the whole story, but fearing my reaction. She had been so honest with me up to this point, revealing her faults as well as my father's. I knew it had been hard because human nature compels us to cast ourselves in the best light possible, and the American psyche pities the victim. But my trust in her was inherent.

I wanted her to continue, so I waited quietly.

"My sister and my husband were together," she reported with unusual calm. "The betrayal I felt was more than I could bear. Those miscellaneous others were just that, but those two brought the filth into my home, and it broke me. The next day, I went to Dr. Hunter with my mind set on payback. We met for lunch in the restaurant of the Chestnut Hill Hotel, and I had every intention of getting my revenge by giving him, another black man, my body upstairs in a room I had already reserved. But when I took him upstairs, all I could do was cry. And he folded his honey brown arms around me, and he held me until I fell asleep. And that was my guilty pleasure. That I had found comfort and fallen asleep in another man's arms. My actions were not the same, but still bad," she said gravely.

"What do you think of your sweet old mother now?" she asked, turning red-rimmed eyes on me.

I leaned over and kissed her on the forehead before I got up to go in the house.

home

I thought it strange that I wasn't sure whether to knock or use my key, but as I stood on the steps wondering, my dad opened the door, looking at me strangely.

"Hi," he said, opening the screen door.

"Hey," I responded, stepping inside.

The house was a shell. The paintings had been removed from their spaces on the walls, and they sat on the floor, wrapped in brown paper and bubble wrap. The sconces and other decorative touches that my mother had bought but not taken with her were piled in boxes marked "foyer" plopped around the floor.

"Wow! You've been busy, huh?" I said, wavering between my usual "everything-is-just-dandy" enthusiasm and my natural self.

"Mm-hmm. There was a lot to do. Do you think that your mother wants any of that stuff?" he asked, gesturing toward the boxes spilling tangible memories.

"I don't think so," I said as I moved into the living room to look around. "She's pretty well set up."

"Yeah, I imagine she would be," he replied, settling into his music chair. "What about you? Are you okay?"

I was surprised that he asked. He never had before, but given all that had happened, it was a natural question.

Anxious to dismiss the question, I shrugged and said, "I guess. Are you going to be alright down there in the country?"

"Hampton's not that country. You've got Norfolk, Virginia Beach, and the bases all around, not to mention the university. It's slower and more relaxed than Philly. I'm looking forward to it."

"Oh," I said, again at a loss for words. "Well, I'll go check out my room."

I treaded the stairs slowly, as if somehow afraid of what I'd find at the top. The door to my room was closed, and I feared opening. I breathed deeply and did it. Although I'd been to the house over the years, I'd never gone upstairs. At first I thought I'd been giving my father his privacy, but then I realized that I had been distancing myself from this place that hadn't felt like a home in years.

The room was exactly the same as when I'd lived there. Nothing had been touched. The only additions were the flattened packing boxes that lay on the bed. It was as if he had been waiting for me to come back. I stepped inside the black-and-white room. Diverse faces from magazine ads for United Colors of Benetton hung on the wall, staring at me through slanted and round eyes. Black-and-white panels of sheer fabric hung from high windows and from bars on top of the canopy bed. Endless strings of pearls cascaded from the doorknobs and the backs of chairs around the room. The dresser was strewn with the half-empty bottles of perfume that I had loved so much during high school. The black leather Africa medallion that had been popularized by some 1980s rappers sat on my desk next to a copy of Conrad's *Heart of Darkness* and Haley's *The Autobiography of Malcolm X*. I searched the dresser drawers, unearthing a blend of lacy bras and androgynous tank tops. The closet revealed a mix of sacklike black clothes and a few small dresses shoved in the corner near the back. The room was a confusing array of moods, and the mix was overwhelming.

Visually sweeping the room again, I numbly mumbled, "He didn't do a thing."

The words stuck on my lips, and I repeated them. "He didn't do a thing."

Suddenly I was besieged by images of myself racing about in a blind rage trying to get him to notice me. That's what it had all been for. For him to speak those three words to me. For him to tell me what I needed to hear. That he loved me. All of those poor decisions, all of those bloody lines on the insides of my arms, all of those thoughts wafting up in smoke like burning sacrifices to Apollo, all of those assaults hurled at me by Lionel, all of those faceless anonymous men pushing themselves inside of me were his fault. They were all for him, and he had done nothing to rescue me from myself or to protect me from others.

A cry burst forth from my throat at the same time the tears hit. He appeared in the doorway and regarded me, the monster he had helped create, with horror. I pushed past him, screaming my pain, and raced down the stairs and toward the door, tripping over the boxes and paintings along the way.

"Shanna," I heard him call behind me.

But it was too late. I was out the door, running toward my car. I jumped in, slamming the door and starting the car simultaneously. I could hear him running down the steps after me, but I was gone before he could get to the sidewalk. I whipped the car out of the driveway and peeled off down the street, but I didn't know where to go, and that made me wail even harder. I had no place to go, so I pulled over before I got to Lincoln Drive because I knew that I would never make it to the end of that snaky drive. On the side of the road, I hacked and heaved until there was nothing left in me, no tears, no food, nothing. Then I drove back to my father's house to explain, to try to make some sense of my emotions, but he was gone.

looking for lionel 2

I whipped my Mercedes Kompressor through the streets of North Philadelphia for hours, trying to find Lionel to undo the grief and guilt that was eating away at my heart. For hours and hours I drove, unsure of what I would do if I found him. As darkness fell over the city, I felt myself plunging deeper and deeper into chaos, chasing a phantom with hopes that I would be exorcised and finally find peace. Through the neighborhoods I went, crisscrossing the streets like the bloody plaid of my great-grandmother's stomach and the healed but hurting lines on the insides of my arms. I wanted to find him and take him back to his mother so that she could love him back to health. I wanted to find him and bring him back to the Main Line with me so that he could dry out in a comfortable and discreet detox center. I wanted to find him and love him deeply and truly this time, and I would appreciate the stuff that made him, him. I just wanted to find him, and no amount of sleep could remove him from my mind.

under the ivy awning

I listened to her as she spoke, continuing to fill in the background of the painting that was my life.

"On our fifth anniversary, your father woke me up with breakfast in bed and a kiss. He had sliced some strawberries, bananas, and kiwi for me. He'd made some cheesy grits, which he introduced me to, and I'm still addicted to them. He boiled an egg for me, cut out the yolk, and sprinkled salt on the white. And he spread gooseberry jam on a scone and placed an edible flower on top. To this day, that was the best breakfast that I've ever had," she reported smiling.

Then she was quiet, reflecting.

"I still love him," she whispered into the blackness of the night.

graham england

I stepped into his office at *Philly* magazine, and he was seated behind his desk. With his glasses perched on his nose, he looked much older than he had looked when I'd met him at the anniversary party.

"Shanna, I'm glad you called," Graham England said, smiling brightly as I approached. "You had crossed my mind, and I was thinking that you'd be great to shoot the photos for this article that I've got coming. Come. Have a seat," he offered, motioning toward the sofa.

"Can I get you anything?" he asked.

"No, I'm fine, thanks. Mom and I are meeting for lunch in a little while," I said.

"Your mom is a gem. I love that lady," he commented, reaching for the portfolio on my lap. "May I?"

"Of course," I said, unzipping the portfolio and opening it.

As he flipped quickly through the pages, I felt strangely connected to the photos. Each one was like a little piece of my life. From the nature shots and the Kelly Drive athletes to the kids in North Philly and the candid shots of local dignitaries, they were all things that had come through my eyes and been temporarily imprinted on my psyche. Vulnerability crept in, almost causing me to snatch the book from him.

I studied his face to distract myself and give me something to do. His skin had a healthy tan to it, and his hair, which fell softly onto his forehead, had blond highlights, professionally done, no doubt, as his Main Line upbringing would dictate. Tiny crow's feet fanned out from his green eyes, which were dancing with delight as he beheld the picture of Uncle Joe proudly holding a head of cabbage from the vegetable garden from behind his house. Graham flashed his capped, startlingly white teeth, and he actually looked pretty handsome.

"Why are you staring at me?" he asked suddenly, not moving his eyes from the portfolio.

"Huh?" I stuttered, caught off guard.

"What's so interesting?"

"Uh, nothing."

"Gee, thanks," he said laughing.

"It's just that it makes me nervous to have someone examining my work."

He was sharp and personable. I wondered if he was the kind of man my mother was supposed to marry. Had they ever dated? He looked up quickly as if reading my thoughts, and I averted my eyes, shifting my gaze to the map of the city on the wall.

"You have a good eye. You should feel nervous only if you didn't," he said, attempting to calm me.

"Thanks."

"I have a writer doing a story on cabdrivers. A human interest piece about how so many of them are immigrants who arrived in the City of Brotherly Love . . ."

"And Sisterly Affection," I interjected coyly.

"That's cute," he smiled. "Well they come to Philly from a lot of places, Africa, the Middle East, etcetera, looking to start over. The writer is going to tell some of their stories, follow a few of them for a day or two, and get their reactions to the assaults on cabbies that have been happening lately. I want you to capture their humanity. It's one thing to photograph them outside of 30th Street Station, hustling for customers. A shot like that would be aesthetically pleasing with its neat lines and the monochromatic and geometric look of the yellow cabs all lined up. But I want you to do something different. Capture a guy scarfing down a bite to eat between runs. Show a guy helping an old lady out of a cab. Do you get what I'm saying?"

"I do."

"I thought you would. Good. The pay is seventy-five dollars per photo, and I'm looking to use about six or seven. Sound okay to you?"

"Absolutely," I replied, trying to conceal my excitement.

"Okay. I need to get back to work and you need to meet your mom. I'm looking forward to working with you."

"Me too, Graham. Thanks so much."

"Don't thank me yet. I can be a real hard-ass."

"You're trying to run a respectable magazine."

He smiled at me, his eyes still twinkling. "My receptionist has your independent contractor agreement and a few other documents you'll need to sign. Get them back to her before the week's out," he said, rising and taking my hand.

"Okay. I'll be in touch. Bye, Graham," I said, resting my hand in his.

"Bye, Shanna."

On the other side of the door, I breathed a sigh of relief and smiled, hoping that this would be a new beginning for me.

disclosure

As a child, I had had so many questions for my mother. She had answered many of them during our evening talks on the patio, but still I had more. I had wanted to know why she had made some of the choices she had made, like leaving me, and if she'd regretted it.

So one evening I began to ask her the questions that had been burned into my brain all of those years ago, and she answered me with candor, and I appreciated it.

"Why did you leave me?"

She sighed before answering. "I was dizzy with grief most of the time, like I was in a constant funeral procession, and the deceased was my heart. Most days, I felt like my soul had been sucked out of me because your dad was so grim and dour with me. He loved you, though, and I thought that you'd be okay with him."

"But that doesn't answer why you left. Was I that bad?"

"No, sweetie, I didn't leave because of you. I left because I was selfish. And I've paid for it every day since then."

I was quiet as I attempted to absorb her explanation. Minutes crept by like hours before I asked my next question.

"Why did you leave the Main Line?"

"I left for love."

"Was that all?"

"Mostly."

"Were you purposely leaving something behind?"

"I was intentionally leaving everything behind. It was too complicated when what I needed was simplicity."

"Why didn't you ever go back?"

"I didn't want to. It looked like I was hiding out, but it wasn't really like that. Mt. Airy was a refuge for me at a time when I really needed it, so I was happy to be there. I grew up in this very house, but after a while it was suffocating me, and I needed to leave it."

"Why didn't you bring me here when I was a child?"

"Because it wouldn't have been your home. This place has not always been so open, and I didn't want you to feel the hurt of it."

"Why didn't any of your old friends come around to visit?"

"Because I didn't want them to. I couldn't engage in their shallow discussions and futile discourses when I had a daughter to raise. They could, but I couldn't."

"Did you ever want to come back?"

"From time to time."

"Sometimes I would catch you crying. Why did you cry?"

"Because I have a woman's heart, and a woman's heart always feels grief and guilt even when she can't put her finger on the reason."

"Did you ever feel trapped with us?"

"Never. You were my world, and I wanted to be with you even when I wasn't."

"Did you ever have any dreams?"

"Honey, Main Line women don't dream. We simply are. We're raised to marry well, and that's what we do with our daughters. We raise them to marry well, but we never really define what 'well' is. It means monied, but that's it. In between being raised and raising our children, or looking on as the nanny does, we volunteer for a distant charity, we play tennis, we vacation from jobs we don't have, and we focus on being thin, pretty, and charming."

"Did you ever love anyone before my Dad?"

"No, baby. And I haven't loved anyone since."

cabbies

It took me almost a week to do it, but at the end, I knew that it was perfect. The drivers I met were surprisingly accommodating. Once I explained what I was doing, and after they compared notes on the rumors they had heard about a story being done on foreign cab-drivers, many offered to be my guides.

I arrived at Amtrak's 30th Street Station at seven one morning. After parking my car in the garage under the train station, I emerged into the brilliance of the sun and plopped myself on a marble and stone flowerpot that doubled as a barricade. I fished through my bag for my press credentials, and I watched the boisterous dark figures talking animatedly to each other. I looked for the most subdued driver near the front of the line, and I jotted down his license plate number, cab company, and car number. After calling it in to Graham's answering voicemail, I approached him smiling. I flashed my credentials and showed him my camera before introducing myself. He returned my smile, white teeth glowing against the smooth black-ness of his face. He said his name was Fasika, and he was from Somalia. As I began explaining what I was doing, he nodded, like he was familiar with my story. Then we leaned against the cab, waiting for the daily influx of out-of-towners and Center City commuters to make their way toward us.

I rode with him as he made his way around the city. The route was like an exercise in connecting the dots. I wanted to warm Fasika up, and the perfect opportunity presented itself to me. With each new passenger I had a new opportunity to fabricate a story to explain why I was riding shotgun.

"Hi. I'm Tara Smith, and I'm accompanying Fasika to make sure he complies with the city's new safety regulations."

"Hi there. My name is Susan Williams, and I'm Fasika's supervisor. I've gotten some complaints about his driving, so I'm here to analyze for myself."

"Hola. My name is Maria, and I just felt like coming to work with my man today."

He laughed at every lie, giving me perfect photo opportunities, his bright smile like the sun shining through the clouds. I clicked away, never bothering to explain the camera to the passengers.

Start at 30th Street, go to 18th and Market, stop. Start at 12th Street, go to 53rd and Walton, stop. Start at 54th and Osage, go to the numbers house at 58th and Baltimore, then to the dry cleaner at 48th and Spruce, then the check cashing place at 46th and Locust, then "damn-can't-you-understand-English-I-said-44th-and-Locust," then back to 54th and Osage. Start at 48th and Chestnut, go to 21st and Walnut, then "damn-I-don't-have-my-money-on-me-wait-right-here," then nothing, then a disgusted shrug and cursing in a language I don't understand, but I capture the universally spoken frustration on his face.

At ten thirty Fasika pulled the cab over as we cruised the business strip of a residential community and asked me if I was ready for lunch.

"It's still early," I said, mildly perplexed.

"It's either now or two o'clock," he responded, moving to open the door.

I nodded and began to gather my things. I followed his movements, camera in hand, catching him in midstretch, unfolding his body, and reaching jauntily toward the sky. As if he soaked in energy through his fingertips, he began walking so quickly I nearly sprinted to keep up with him.

He entered a Middle Eastern vegetarian restaurant where he ordered a falafel sandwich with a side of fries and a bottle of water. I did the same and reached in my bag for my wallet, saying, "Allow me."

Fasika looked at me with his top lip curled in a mix of scorn and amusement before shaking his head and mumbling, "American women."

Not eager to engage in a discussion on the politics of gender with a man who knew nothing of me or my circumstances, I let the remark slide. He had moved halfway around the world in search of a better life for his family. He couldn't possibly understand the motivation of a woman whose mother had been raised to be a princess and whose father raised her to be a mule.

After praying, he hunched over his food as if someone were going to sneak up behind him and snatch it. He began to gobble it, but when he saw me rest my camera on the table, he forced himself to slow down.

"Do what you normally do," I said.

His eyes laughed as he said, "Normally I eat in the car. I'm trying to be civil."

"Well, back to the car it is," I said, shoving a few fries in my mouth and wrapping the rest of my falafel pita in the wax paper that lined the tray.

Ignoring my movement, he scarfed down the rest of his food and went to the restroom. We strolled out to the car and before he got in, he raised his face to the sun and sucked in the open air once more before stuffing his body back into the car. As I snapped his picture, I wondered if that's what the slaves must have felt before being crammed below the deck of a slave ship.

For the rest of the week I followed a few more drivers, capturing telling shots of them rushing to relieve themselves in alleyways between runs, squeezing family members in for quick trips to doctors' offices and other appointments, and zipping around the city in a rush to rack up fares that would feed families on two continents. America was their hustling ground, and they were determined to make it work for them.

At the close of the week I assembled a large group of drivers at 30th Street Station. Each wore a light-colored tunic or T-shirt, dark pants, and sandals. At sunrise each leaned on his car, facing the east, and I stood atop the stone-and-marble planter, rising like a sun goddess, and I snapped pictures of the dark faces of smiling men, warming under the sun that singed them at home but shone pure hope here in America.

boiling

Even though I've listened to her words, heard her explanations, anger still eats away at me from time to time. I'm trying to wrap myself in forgiveness, but still I hurt. I hurt when I think of the years I wasted feeling empty, and the hours I squandered trying to fill the vacuum. I think of how it all could have been avoided if she had just listened to my father when he'd warned her. Her own desires were more important then, and she echoed that sentiment when she abandoned us, me, and fled back here. She's right. She was selfish, and I can't escape feeling that even now, as she's nurturing me and bringing me into her world, that she's trying to appear selfless. And that's selfish, too.

looking for lionel iii

I laid the large yellow envelope in the center of my bed and sifted through the mound that lay before me. Pictures of Lionel looking innocent, ambitious, and angry all at once faced me. Under the pictures lay stationery as thick as cotton, and under that lay a pile of twenty-dollar bills. I was hoping that the density of the wad of money would camouflage the seemingly flimsy nature of my intentions. It was part of a payoff. Ransom for a soul already assumed lost.

On the cotton-thick paper, I scrawled the words "He always loved you more" in black ink. I wrapped the note around the bills and stuffed them into an envelope. Lifting the stack of pictures, I traced Lionel's lips and thought of the irony of lips so soft that they could pleasure a woman through multiple orgasms but also wrap themselves around a wad of spit aimed at the same woman. I shrugged and sucked back tears before stuffing the pictures and money and note into the large yellow envelope.

I maneuvered my car stealthily down the familiar, narrow street, throwing the flashers on and hopping out to hurry up the broken concrete stairs. Opening the creaking screen door, I slid the envelope underneath the opening between the floor and the storm door. Withdrawing quickly when I saw a television's blue light reflecting on the floor, I rushed back toward my car and sped off down the street momentarily relieved for having tithed my share of guilt money.

exchanges

"Graham told me about the fabulous job that you did on the pictures for the magazine," my mother said beaming.

"Yeah, he seemed to like them when I showed them to him. He originally said that he'd use six or seven, but he liked them so much that he's going to use eight in the spread," I explained.

"Great, honey. When do I get to see them?"

"When the magazine comes out," I quipped, laughing before I dived into the salmon Caesar salad I'd brought home from Center City where I'd gone on a preliminary scouting mission for my next assignment. I was going to take photos for an exposé on teen prostitution, and I'd started cruising south of Market around 13th Street, the section of the city where homosexuals abounded. I knew that there would be a strong chance of finding teenage boys peddling their bodies there, half for experimentation, half for financial need because many were runaways. Graham had also suggested some sections in Kensington, West Philly, and North Philly, but I mentally declined going to North Philly. Its residents had been exploited enough on the nightly news and didn't need any more notoriety, especially in print.

As if reading my thoughts, my mother said, "What's Graham got you working on next?"

"A story on teenage prostitution," I responded.

"That's rather morbid and draining, isn't it?"

Her tone sounded almost dismissive, and I consciously fought to quell the defensiveness I felt rising in me. She didn't know that I had made similar exchanges as I fought the emptiness that threatened me. Only I hadn't charged. My fee was paid in words. I simply nodded and began picking with my salad, pushing hunks of romaine lettuce from side to side.

After a prolonged silence, I spoke. "Did you ever have a thing for Graham?"

She laughed before saying, "We dated off and on through high school. I wouldn't let it get serious, though."

"Why? It probably would have been easier on you."

"Well, Graham's nice and all, but he's always been very white bread."

"What do you mean?"

"He's good-looking and accomplished and all, but he's always been very straight."

"What's wrong with straight?" I inquired.

"Nothing, if that's your taste."

"So what's yours?" I snapped, knowing that I wouldn't like what would follow and feeling myself get angry.

"I always liked guys with more texture. More grit."

"Oh, you mean you've always liked a little edge. Nothing like a little thug passion to spice up your bland, white bread, Main Line life, huh? That's where my father came in, huh?"

"Shanna, don't you dare. I loved your father."

"You sure had a funny way of showing it. Swoop down from your castle on high to play with the natives for a while, live life on the edge, produce a little mulatto bastard like whites have done all over the world, then leave your grimy man and your mixed up child before returning to your palace on high."

"Shanna, I wanted you. Your father didn't."

"Well, maybe he was on to something. He knew what a strain it would be for half a man to raise a whole child. You, on the other hand, didn't even try," I shouted, shoving myself back from the table.

"Shanna, don't," she whimpered, tears spilling out of her eyes onto her reddening face.

"Y'all saved me, and for what? Nothing. Nothing but misery. I hope you had a good time while your walk on the wild side lasted," I ranted, knocking over the chair as I scrambled up and rushed into the house where I grabbed my camera, purse, and keys. I slammed the door as I exited the castle, shattering the calm quiet of the community as I peeled out of the driveway.

that night

That night I drove to the liquor store where I bought a bottle of vodka. Then I drove to one of the parking lots on West River Drive where I sat on the hood of the car. I sipped my way through a third of the bottle while the strained, beautiful voice of Marvin Gaye drifted out to me from the powerful Bose speakers. Again I was wrapped in his pain as he sang about falling apart.

I heard him croon in his raspy-edged falsetto, and I swallowed more of the clear liquid. I'd missed the taste of the alcohol, and I chastised myself for staying away for so long while trying to make nice and play normal when there was nothing normal about me.

"Tell me about it, Marvin," I yelled into the darkness. Rules were what the powerful made up to keep the masses in line. And that shit worked. The masses wasted their lives chasing a dollar and a dream while trying to stay within the lines, while the rich played the game their way, flipping the bird at the rules every chance they got.

As Marvin sang about the three things in life that are sure, I clapped in agreement. Trouble. That's what I was. That's what I'd always been. The sight of my face had bedeviled my father from the start. Then, my existence was too much for my mother, so she'd left. Then, my presence in school had irked the hell out of my classmates, and they'd let me know. Then, Lionel. Then, his son's mother.

"God, why did you put me here?" I wailed, falling back onto the hood. I sucked on the bottle again, holding the liquid in my cheeks as long as possible before swallowing it as Marvin concluded, his voice fading into the night.

I pulled the car out of the parking lot and aimed it toward West Philly, the once middle-class enclave that had been crushed by heroin. After parking in a church lot, I grabbed my gear and headed toward 52nd Street, the business strip lined with shopkeepers and Muslim street merchants selling incense and oils among other things.

I scoped the crowded street, scanning it for young, vulnerable faces hardened by the pressure of life on the streets. Then, a youngish girl with a ridiculous-looking Lil' Kim weave appeared. Garbed in skimpy shorts, a halter top, and clunky, high-heeled sandals, she sidled up to a neatly dressed man who was pulling down the grated gate on a storefront. She leaned in to whisper something to him, and he nodded, whispering something back before he smiled nastily. She moved away, attempting to switch seductively, but half-tripping over the chunky heels of her shoes. He watched her smiling before pulling the gate all the way down and bending down to lock it. He stood, smoothing his pants and adjusting his crotch before walking off in the same direction as the little girl.

I followed him down the street, needing to capture the scene on film, but wanting to stop what I knew would happen.

"Save that little girl from herself," my heart wanted my mouth to shout, but I knew that if not him, she would lure someone else into the alleyway where she would squat to her knees like she was doing now. The merchant leaned back against the wall while she unfastened his pants in the dark like a pro. The streetlamp at the other end of the alley provided the perfect lighting for the silhouette of her taking him into her mouth. I snapped away, finishing just as he did, and

I hurried back into the light, not wanting to witness the exchange of money.

I sadly captured multiple scenes of the same sort in different sections of the city, and as the hours crept by, I wondered if any of the girls' parents wondered where they were. I wept for them from the safety of my car, for they were worth weeping for.

After I finished my rounds, at midnight I called Graham's house from an upscale jazz restaurant in a Center City hotel.

"Hello," he chirped, sounding wide awake.

"I'm glad I didn't wake you, Graham. It's Shanna."

"Hi, Shanna," he said, politely waiting for an explanation for my late-night call.

"I, uh, just finished the photos for the new photo shoot, and I just wanted to give you the film."

"I'm in no rush, dear. Hold on to it until you develop them."

"Graham, I'd prefer to get them off my hands tonight."

"Okay," he replied hesitantly. "Where should I meet you?"

"I'm at the Bellevue. I'll meet you in the lobby."

"Alright. I'll see you in twenty. You're okay, aren't you?"

"I'm fine," I said softly. "See you soon."

He found me sitting on a loveseat with my head back and my eyes closed, drained from everything I had seen and heard that day.

"Hey."

"Hey," I responded, hoping that the reek of vodka that I smelled was imaginary.

"You look like you had a rough night," he said, smiling his capped-tooth smile.

"It's not easy watching a fourteen-year-old give a grown-ass man a blow job in an alley."

"Yeah, I guess," he said, sitting next to me. "Your pictures will help save some of them, though."

My mouth twisted in the way that people do when they're doubt-ful, but they don't want to fully express it. I handed him the rolls of film, and he shook the white canisters before stuffing them into his pants pocket.

"Let me walk you to your car. You look tired. Are you going to be okay driving home?"

"I'm not going home tonight," I said, closing my eyes and resting my head on the loveseat again.

"If I may be so bold, where are you going?" he asked.

"With you," I replied opening my eyes.

"My girlfriend's there," he said, laughing before stopping to search my face.

I bit my lip, saying nothing but pleading for human kindness with my eyes.

"I'll be back," he said, getting up to walk to the reception desk. He looked back at me pensively before handing the desk clerk some bills from his wallet. When the agent handed him the key envelope, I got up and headed toward the elevator.

We stepped inside, and he pushed the button for floor number five. We rode up in silence, and he led the way into the room and opened the door with trembling hands.

Inside, he clicked on the light and turned to me.

"Shanna, you don't have to do this. It's not part of the . . ." His voice trailed off as I pressed my mouth to his, using my tongue to part his lips and not caring if he minded the taste of vodka. I kept kissing him as I unbuttoned his shirt and slid his pants from his hips. I pushed him onto the bed where he lay watching me as I dis-robed before silently offering him my body in exchange for a place to stay. Just like the little girls I'd photographed just hours before.

He fucked me gently, and when he finished, guilt made him avert his eyes. He showered quickly and threw on his clothes, shaking his head and muttering, "Liddy Wadsworth would kill me if she knew what I'd just done."

In my sleepy haze, my heart stopped when I heard the name he uttered. Liddy Wadsworth. Wadsworth.

"Be good, kid." He leaned over to kiss me once more. "Here. Get yourself something to eat in the morning," he said, peeling off five twenty-dollar bills and slapping them on the dresser.

"Food doesn't cost that much, and my photos cost more than that. What are you paying for?" I asked rhetorically, turning away from him and curling into a fetal position but not before seeing him grimace.

I closed my eyes and heard the door close.

revelations

I dragged myself into the mansion, wanting nothing more than to climb the stairs and go to my room where I'd crawl into bed and sleep the hurt in my heart away. My mother was pacing in the grand foyer, eyes puffy, looking worse than I'd ever seen her. I didn't pity her, though. I couldn't.

"I'm glad Graham cared enough to call me to tell me where you were. Obviously you aren't that thoughtful."

"I'm surprised he could see the phone to dial the numbers. I fucked him until his eyes bled."

"Shanna!" she gasped, tired eyes open at full mast. She charged toward me with unsure steps, faltering when I turned my angry eyes on her.

"So, Mom, or should I say Liddy Wadsworth, tell me about your father and your family."

Her sagging shoulders suddenly squared, and her chin went up defiantly. "You already figured it out," she spat.

"You tell me. Tell me the story from your perspective, the white perspective."

"You're my child. I don't have to explain anything to you."

"I am your black child, and you owe me everything."

She sat down on the sofa, wringing her hands like Lady Macbeth and looking very small. Her thin lips quivered and her shoulders shook. As I regarded her, I thought of the eternal Southern belle, Scarlett O'Hara, as her world was crashing in around her. Then, the words of Rhett Butler flashed through my head, and, looking at this shaken woman, my mother, I nearly said, "Frankly, my dear, I don't give a damn."

"My father was the younger of two sons of a Virginia landowner. His older brother, Howard, had fought in World War I. He must have seen some terrible things there because my father, Paul, said he wasn't the same when he returned. Like his brain had been fried and all of his guts had been taken out. Howard was ten years older than my dad, and my dad was pretty young at the time, so he didn't really remember much about him. All he knew was that he had ridden to town with his mother, and when they came back, my grandfather was crawling around in the dirt in front of the house and crying something awful. My father ran in the house, and he saw blood splattered all over the wall of the parlor where his brother had blown his head off. My father said he never forgot the sight of his brother's body with his legs tangled in the chair he had fallen off of.

"My father stayed on the farm through the Depression. He said it was like everything died then. Not just crops, but everybody's spirits, too. He said he had to get out of there, so he left Virginia with one suitcase and five thousand dollars. He came to Philadelphia in 1941, and he bought the first property he saw for sale while coming from the train station, a small apartment house in North Philadelphia. Black people were still coming north in droves, so he rented out the apartments, and by year's end he bought another building, a larger one.

"By year's end, he also got word from home about what had happened on the family farm. He rushed back down there to see what he could do, but the rest of that family, your family, had already moved on. The word was that they had gone over to Hampton, and my father said that he wanted to go visit them. He said that he'd never had any truck, that's Southern for trouble, with them, and, in fact, he'd liked the twins, especially the boy. My grandmother told my father that visiting wouldn't make a difference. What's done was done, so my father turned around and headed back to Philadelphia.

"Business was great, and he bought a boatload of properties the following year, venturing into commercial real estate in Center City. He joined a country club and bought a house, but he still hadn't put down any roots, and he was open to it. Finding a wife wasn't difficult for him at all. He married the young daughter of one of the country club members. Mother was almost twenty years his junior. She got pregnant right away, and he named my brother after his own brother, Howard. Then, he named me after his mother. He let mother pick my sister's name.

"We moved into this house in 1955 and we lived well, joining the same country club where my parents had met, taking riding lessons, making our debut, attending private schools, and occasionally volunteering in the city. Then I went off to Brown, met your father, and we got married. After we married, I brought your father here to meet my family. I knew that the order in which I did things went against the order in which I was supposed to do them. My father called it putting the cart before the horse. Then, add in the fact that your dad is black, and it made a difficult situation even worse."

"I thought you said that your father liked my grandmother and her brother," I said skeptically.

"Liking them was one thing. Having blacks in the family was a different story, and my father told me so. He said he recognized your

197

father the minute he walked in the door. He didn't say that to your father. That would have been crass, like Archie Bunker, and that sort of behavior is not Main Line, nor is it Southern for that matter. While your father waited right here on this sofa, my father took me in his study and told me the story. He said that your dad looked just like his uncle and his grandfather. He didn't say that to your father. As he told me the story, he didn't look well. He wasn't well. He was old, but this was the last thing he needed. He swore me to secrecy. I told him it wasn't his fault, kissed him good-bye, and left the house. He had a heart attack that evening, and he died before I got to the hospital. And that was that."

"Did you ever tell my father that your grandfather murdered his grandfather?"

"No," she whispered. "I'd planned never to tell him, but I guess it's out of my hands now, huh?"

I knew what she was asking me. She was asking me not to tell, but I wouldn't be a party to her lies. Generations had passed and blood had thinned, but lies were still lies and murder was still murder. There was no gray space between black and white with this. Her grandfather was a murderer, and generations later, she still had blood on her hands.

I walked up the stairs to my bedroom where I packed my overnight bag for Virginia. I was leaving behind all of the designer suits and ensembles she had bought me, packing only jeans, T-shirts, and cargo pants. I left all of the jewelry on the dresser.

I dug in my desk drawer for the card that my dad had mailed to me with his new address and telephone number. When I found it, I shoved it in my purse, gathered up my camera and accessories, and walked out of the bedroom, closing the door behind me.

When I descended the stairs, I saw that my mother was still sitting where I'd left her, looking thin and pale. As I said good-bye, she spoke to me of guilt and forgiveness, but I couldn't hear her. She reached out to hug me, but I couldn't hug back.

"Shanna, if you're going to go, at least wait until the rain stops," she begged.

"Good-bye, Liddy," I responded, stepping outside and heading toward my car, not bothering to shield my head from the rain.

With racing heart,
I drove through rain,
Anxious to see
My dad again.
I'd called him once
From Delaware
Told him by sunset
I'd be there.
He seemed happy
To hear my voice
Was glad I'd grown
And made the choice
To spend some time
Staying with him
Getting to know
His Southern kin
Said, "Great." Planned to
Hang up the phone.
He said, "Wait, Shanna,
Please hold on.

Always wanted
To tell you this
Embrace you tight
Give you a kiss,
Say 'I love you,
You are my world,
So happy you're
My little girl.' "
I said, "Thanks, Dad.
I love you, too.
Needed to hear
Those words from you.
I'll be there soon,
Something to tell.
Exonerate
Your mom from hell."
He said, "Okay,
Be careful. Bye."
Rain still streaming
Down from the sky.
Wash sins away
New start for me.
No Lionel, Liddy
Just dad and me.
Reached for a tissue
To blow my nose
Hit the slick spot
There on the road.
I hydroplaned
And hit a tree

No seat belt
Old habit, you see.
The doors weren't locked
Flew from the car
Lay unconscious
On the black tar.
Hours like minutes
They flew on by
Felt my body
Ascend toward sky
The sun had set
And there I lay
Won't see my dad,
No not today
Floating toward
The softest light
No longer trapped
Between black and white.

reading group companion
for
Floating
by Nicole Bailey-Williams

1. Many of us have moments when we realize that we are different, and often with that realization comes alienation. When does Shanna's "moment of awakening" regarding her racial identity come? Is it more harmful for her because she is so young when it happens?

2. In "Cooling," Shanna reveals that her feelings for Lionel have evolved from the fiery intensity that she initially felt to a malevolent passiveness. What draws her to him initially? What does she see in him that makes her romantic feelings begin to subside?

3. Readers are introduced to "the four fathers" through Shanna's father, James, in the vignette "Rememory." What are the lessons that they teach him? Are their lessons demonstrated through his actions? How does his mother counteract the strength that they attempt to instill in him? What are some lessons that you have learned from co-parents, mentors, or family friends?

4. In "Going Home," Shanna begins to learn about her father's family history. How does learning about her past help to ground her, empowering her to make some choices that are beneficial to her?

5. In Part Three, Shanna goes to live with her mother in the affluent Main Line world. She likens the experience to being reborn. In what ways are her eyes opened for the first time? What experiences are new for her? Is she emotionally ready for her new life?

6. Through James, Shanna's father, readers come to view his mother as manipulative. Does Elizabeth, Shanna's mother, demonstrate that or any other characteristics that are similar?

7. Throughout American literature, readers have met numerous literary figures who are classified as tragic mulatto figures, those whose biracial or multiracial identity confuses them. How does Shanna fit that classification? How does she differ? Does she have a "break out" moment in which she is clear about who she is?

8. Shanna is plagued by feelings of abandonment that stem from her mother's desertion. These abandonment issues resurface in other areas of her life. How does she try to make amends in her desertion of Lionel?

9. Shanna's father is very aware of his shortcomings, and he demonstrates honesty in revealing those flaws to others. How do his needs get overlooked in his relationship with Elizabeth? How does he attempt to move beyond his human frailties in order to reach out to Shanna?

10. James, Shanna, and Elizabeth all have pasts that haunt them; however, knowledge of the past reveals important facts about both family and personal history. What is some information that you have learned that you wish you had known sooner? What is something that you'd rather not have learned? How did this knowledge change you?

Author of the acclaimed novel *A Little Piece of Sky* (Harlem Moon, 2002), NICOLE BAILEY-WILLIAMS is a high school English teacher and cohost of *The Literary Review*, a Philadelphia radio show. Her writing has appeared in a variety of publications, including *Publishers Weekly*, *Black Issues Book Review*, and *Gumbo: An Anthology of African American Writing*. She lives in Philadelphia.